EBURY PRESS
# AGHORI 2

A motivational speaker, leadership coach and behavioural trainer by profession, Mayur Kalbag's hobby of writing poetry and prose evolved into a serious avocation twelve years ago, after he returned from a trip to Kailash Mansarovar along with his guru, Swami Sadyojat Shankarashram.

Mayur has written two books of poetry: *Smile at Stress* and *Rising Waterfall*. His first book of prose, *Adventures of Poorna*, was well received by readers.

Mayur is also a passionate artist and has made his mark in the abstract as well as contemporary genre with art exhibitions in India and Switzerland.

An adventurer at heart, Mayur is an avid trekker and rock climber.

Apart from all this, his true passion is imagining, visualizing, exploring and then articulating new realms of philosophical fiction and spiritualism through the process of writing.

# Aghori 2

## THE UNTOLD STORY
## CONTINUES

# MAYUR KALBAG

EBURY
PRESS

An imprint of Penguin Random House

EBURY PRESS

Ebury Press is an imprint of the Penguin Random House group of companies
whose addresses can be found at global.penguinrandomhouse.com

Published by Penguin Random House India Pvt. Ltd
4th Floor, Capital Tower 1, MG Road,
Gurugram 122 002, Haryana, India

Penguin
Random House
India

First published in Ebury Press by Penguin Random House India 2024

ISBN 9780143465201

Typeset in Sabon LT Std by Manipal Technologies Limited, Manipal
Printed at Thomson Press India Ltd, New Delhi

www.penguin.co.in

*The love and guidance of my guru, Swami Sadyojat Shankarashram, along with the teachings He has imparted to me, have been the true inspiration for all my passionate pursuits—one of them being writing poetry and prose. Swamiji's love and blessings have been the wind beneath my wings that let me fly to different and unexplored horizons of thoughts and imagination, and truly have enabled me to write my stories and compose my poems. His words of wisdom have been the oxygen to keep my mind vibrantly awakened, and for it to think not just outside the box but above it!*

*I dedicate my book,* Aghori 2: The Untold Story Continues, *to my beloved guru, who means more than the world to me, and whom I love and respect from the depths of my heart.*

# 1

# Aulaakh Niranjan

'*Aulaakh Niranjan.*' The voice sounded familiar!

'Who is he?' I wondered. The voice was not that of any of the Aghori sadhus I had lived with, and yet I felt some familiarity. Even before I could venture an intelligent guess, Swamiji, who was seated next to me, exclaimed, 'Why are you standing away from us? Come and join us!'

I was surprised to see an Aghori sadhu walking towards Swamiji. With each stride, he kept exclaiming at high decibels, '*Aulaakh Niranjan.*' As he came closer, I saw him clearly and my happiness knew no bounds when I realized that this Aghori was none other than Tadamba. I had met him when I was in the Himalayas at my guru's command—the Aghori sadhus had embedded three powerful mantras in me, which would later be extracted and transferred to my guru.

I could not stop myself. I spontaneously stood up and walked towards him. 'I am so happy that you are here. But you could have come with me rather than coming here all alone!' I told him.

Before he could say anything, Swamiji exclaimed aloud, accompanied with hearty laughter, 'Looks like everyone is getting fooled! Even Subbu.'

I was surprised at what my guru had just said, and wasn't sure what was going on.

'He is not who you think he is. He is the twin brother of your beloved Tadamba,' my guru said, and began laughing again, this time with even more gusto. 'Come closer; I wish to formally introduce you to my forever curious disciple.'

Hearing this, the Tadamba lookalike came closer and stood just a foot away from me. He looked at me and gave me a big smile! 'I know you miss Tadamba, but I am not him. I am his brother and my name is Tantrayya. I am here in Shirali at the request of your beloved Swamiji,' he said.

'But I thought you were him! Both of you look the same and your voice sounds just like his,' I reacted quickly.

Swamiji was listening to our conversation with a smile on his face.

'Tantrayya, I have called you here to the *Math* (temple) for a special reason. You have lived and studied at the Sugandha temple at Gulati in Assam. I need an expert like you for this activity and you were recommended especially by the senior Aghori sadhus in the Himalayas.' Swamiji looked at me and continued, 'Subbu, Tantrayya is not only Tadamba's twin brother but more importantly, is a scholar in Tantras. He is one of three students across the globe who has the designation of a *Tantraki* scholar and it is for this reason that I have invited him to our Math.'

These words from Swamiji got me pleasantly confused as I had no idea why my guru had called Tantrayya. I gathered enough courage to speak up, 'Swamiji, is there some reason for calling him here at this time of the year?'

Swamiji looked towards the sky, gazing up for almost two minutes. Then, taking a deep breath, he turned to me and exclaimed in heightened exuberance, 'Tantrayya is here to help with the extraction and the transference of the rare and powerful mantras from you into me! But he is also here for another reason that is as important, if not more. But you do not need to know that now.' Swamiji looked towards the sky again, and this time his gaze was extremely intense. He then looked at Tantrayya, turned to me and exclaimed, this time in a deeper voice, 'Subbu, Tantrayya is arguably the most learned and may I say, the most effective tantric in the world and he has been beckoned here to enable the defeat of Soornayee!'

Hearing this name sent shivers down my spine; shivers of nervousness and fear, for a very good reason. Not only in our village but across the state of Karnataka, she was known as the most powerful and poisonous witch. In fact, there is still a question as to whether she is really a woman or a man!

# 2

# It Has Venom Which It Spews on Its Victim!

A part of me was deeply anguished while another part was in vibrant wonderment regarding this entity. This was the first time I had heard Swamiji mention the name of this witch. 'Subbu, for now, please focus upon the mantra transference from you into me as that is the key to defeating Soornayee. You have always been the curious one, which is why you were sent to the Aghori sadhus and you are equally curious about the witch. Don't worry, Subbu! You will get all your answers about this entity, but that will happen in due time. What you need to do in the coming days is to help us in the extraction of the three significant mantras.'

'Yes, Swamiji,' I replied, albeit with subtle nervousness written over my face.

'Now that you have been introduced to Tantrayya, I feel it is vital that we listen to everything he has to say. Over to you, Tantrayya,' said Swamiji and sat in his regular *Ardha-siddhasana* style.

I was trying my best to sit in the same manner and finally ended up doing it. Seeing my passionate struggle, Tantrayya could not stop smirking.

'Maharaj . . .' Tantrayya started.

'You may address me as Swami or Swamiji just as the others do.'

'Swamiji, at the outset, let me tell you that I feel deeply privileged to have received this blessing to not just meet you but to conduct the important task of extracting and then transferring the three mantras into your body. Having said that, I wish to place in front of you and especially Subbu, the path forward.'

'That is mainly what we want to hear from you,' Swamiji quipped.

'Yes, Swamiji. This is the path. There are three mantras in all, of which the second one is the most critical one and delicate, too, at that. Location-wise, for the extraction and transference of the first one, we have to travel further south as it will have to be done on the banks of the Upasani lake. For the third mantra, we will have to do it here at Shirali, but not inside or near the Math. It will be executed at Alvekoondi beach.'

'What about the second one? Can you tell me and Subbu about that too?' Swamiji asked.

'Yes, Swamiji. As I mentioned before, the second one is going to be the tough one and that is because in the extraction process, a king cobra will be required—I will need Subbu to get bitten by the serpent.'

*Bitten by a cobra and that too a king cobra! Does this mean that I could actually die?* I thought to myself and felt my heart sinking fast. I saw that even Swamiji's facial expressions had changed. He looked confused and a bit upset.

'What do you mean by getting bitten by a snake and a king cobra at that? This is not done! I cannot and will not have Subbu's life being jeopardized for this process.'

Before Swamiji could speak further, Tantrayya turned and looked at me with a wide smile. I smiled back nervously, my fear of getting bitten by a cobra was surely evident.

'Subbu, we will be taking the best possible precautions to ensure that you will not be affected by the venom. Having said that, you will have to go through it for sure—you will have to be bitten by the king cobra. Will you need time to decide or are you fine with this?'

Before I could respond, Swamiji spoke up, 'Tantrayya, this is not going to be an answer that I want Subbu to give now. Let him take a day to think about it. Are you okay with that?'

'Sure, Swamiji! In fact, Subbu can take more than a day. Even a week is fine by me.'

'Subbu! What do you say? Are you ready to have a king cobra bite you?' Swamiji looked towards the sky and smiled.

'Swamiji and Tantrayya, I am very curious about this—about getting bitten, and that too by a snake like the king cobra. But more importantly, I feel blessed to be part of the extraction process. For these reasons, I am willing to do my part in the second extraction process, even if it means giving up my life for it,' I said.

Swamiji suddenly laughed aloud and said, 'Subbu! Please take a day to think properly about it, and then let me and Tantrayya know of your decision.' He paused and added, 'You are not going to die! Right, Tantrayya?'

# 3

# A Hundred Caterpillars

Tantrayya was calm, as though he knew something I did not.

'Yes, Swamiji. I have a feeling that you are aware, but for Subbu, and so that his anxiety and tension will go away, let me explain. Subbu, knowing fully well that the king cobra is probably the most venomous serpent in this world, which can easily put an adult elephant to death with just one bite, can have the most adverse reactions from human beings. However, you need not worry, as I am prepared for this. So, be assured that absolutely nothing will happen to you after the venom enters your body!'

'How is that so? Not only is the king cobra venom one of the most potent ones in the world but the snake has extremely high quantities of it, which it packs into one single bite. How will you ensure that nothing will happen to me?' I asked.

Tantrayya took a deep breath and told one of his assistants to fetch a brown bag that he had kept earlier near a tree. Immediately, the assistant went to the tree, picked up the bag and ever so cautiously held it in his right palm. He brought the bag close to where Tantrayya was standing. Tantrayya prostrated himself before the bag and chanted something softly. I could only see his lips moving but could not hear a word. I was, by now, 100 per cent sure there was a cobra inside the bag. But was there any hissing sound? I supposed the serpent was in *mouna* (silent meditation) and that was probably why it was not hissing.

But to my surprise, there was no serpent inside. After the chanting and prostrations, Tantrayya pulled out what looked like a brown box, and even before I could assume anything, he started making clicking sounds with his tongue and then put the box on the ground. Even Swamiji was watching all of this intently. As the volume of the clicking sounds increased, the lid began to open, seemingly by itself.

'Something strange is inside. Is it something paranormal?' I said in a hushed voice.

'Subbu, this has nothing to do with paranormal entities. You will experience them later. For now, just watch and don't think much.'

Swamiji looked back at Tantrayya and then at the box. In just a few seconds, the lid on that box vanished and what I saw coming out gives me the chills, even till today. Slowly but steadily and in a row, three-inch long caterpillars started crawling out of the box. At least they looked like caterpillars to me. Each one was light green and had lots of tiny hair sprouting from its back. The queue was quite long with each one following another. I was certain these were some kind of insects, but I was unsure as to what they were. By now, nearly fifteen minutes had elapsed and all of them were out of the box.

'Subbu, what you see in front of you are what we call the *sarpendoos*. In your world, these are called caterpillars. But, this is a unique species of caterpillar. It is found only beneath the waters of Mansarovar and nowhere else on this planet,' said Tantrayya.

There was a big question mark painted on my face and I am sure Tantrayya noticed it. 'In case you are wondering why I have brought caterpillars with me, and that too in such large numbers, let me respond. Subbu, I believe in coming prepared whenever and wherever situations such as these arise. So, I have brought anti-venom in the event you agree to being bitten by the king cobra as part of the second mantra extraction,' said Tantrayya. He coolly picked up a couple of caterpillars and came up to me. 'These are and will be your anti-venom!'

# 4

# The Mysterious Sarpendoos

'Wow!' I exclaimed excitedly.

'Could you please explain how these insects will act as an anti-venom remedy?' Swamiji asked.

'Sure, Swamiji. I will explain in detail.'

I was relieved to hear this exchange between Tantrayya and Swamiji.

Tantrayya said, 'These caterpillars aren't the same as all the other ones one typically sees in and around plants and trees. These are different especially because they live at the bottom of lakes and ponds. Unlike others, the sarpendoos, or the *sarpas* as I call them, are the only caterpillars who are carnivorous and feed on venomous serpents. For this very reason, they have been named sarpendoos, and they also have developed resistance to snake venom. Except for sea snakes, the sarpas are completely unaffected by snake bites, especially from cobras and vipers. But the venom does affect them later.'

'What are they going to do for Subbu's bite?' Swamiji asked.

'I was coming to that!' replied Tantrayya. 'These caterpillars, especially the ones I have brought with me, have also developed the strength and the skill to suck venom out from a serpent bite. What the sarpa does is, it enters the bite or the venom-infected area by wriggling its supple body, and starts sucking out the venom-infected blood, which it does through its needle-like fangs. For these caterpillars, the taste is what lures them to suck out all the venom. There is just one concern, and that is the blood that it sucks out to consume the venom. Having said that, you can rest assured that you will be completely free of the venom. With regard to the loss of blood, we will have a few bottles ready for you.'

'Yes, I will have the bottles ready. Just let me know how many you will need,' Swamiji quickly jumped in. 'Will getting your caterpillars into the extraction process be painful for him? If so, then it will be important for him to be mentally prepared,' Swamiji asked Tantrayya with a sense of concern.

'Subbu will feel a slight tingling sensation especially while the sarpas are inside him, but no pain at all,' Tantrayya replied.

'Inside me? Are you saying that these caterpillars will get inside my body?' I asked instantaneously.

'Subbu, it is vital and honestly natural for them to get inside. But you will not feel a thing even though you will be awake and alert. This is mainly due to the anaesthetic-filled saliva they will use to enter your body. In fact, they will enter only that area of your body which has the venom. You will, at the most, feel like someone is gently tickling you. Just see that you don't laugh!' Tantrayya responded with an infectious smile on his face.

I wasn't sure how to react as getting tickled by caterpillars was not something I was truly looking forward to. 'Tantrayya, I have a fundamental question to ask you, particularly because it is you who will be executing the extraction and transference process for all the three mantras. What I wish to ask is, what will be the role of the venom to make the second mantra's extraction successful? And while you are at it, please also explain the processes related to the first and the third extraction.'

Swamiji interrupted to suggest that we all meet again after the evening puja and dinner. 'Are both of you fine with my suggestion or do you wish to continue now itself?' Swamiji asked Tantrayya.

'I think it is better we meet after dinner because I have a lot to explain and it will take a couple of hours at the least,' Tantrayya replied.

'And you must be hungry as well,' Swamiji smilingly responded.

Very honestly, I was keen that Tantrayya continue but Swamiji's suggestion was practical and we all left for our rooms. That evening, I met Tantrayya and his assistants and we went together to join the other temple devotees for the puja.

# 5

# The Mantra and the
# Role of Cobra Venom

After dinner, as planned, Swamiji, his assistant Ratnaiya, Tantrayya, his assistants and I sat in a circle. A chair was kept for Swamiji but he insisted on sitting on the floor like the rest of us.

Tantrayya spoke up, 'Now that we are here, let me start with the role of the king cobra's venom. The serpent that will be participating in this process is a tame one, and to extract the venom, I will be using a thorn from the Sichurai tree. The snake is more like my pet, and I have raised her from the time of her birth. I was keen to bring her with me but due to her large size, I decided to bring her only at the time of the extraction. So, here's what the king cobra bite will do. Once Subbu is bitten, and we will have to ensure this happens on his right wrist, he will start losing sensation from the bite area to his entire body. He will most likely become completely paralysed.

'After this, I will have the caterpillars do their thing and within the next six minutes, Subbu will come back to normality. What is most critical is that, between the time he is bitten till the caterpillars begin their venom extraction, the mantra will be revealed.'

'Revealed?' Swamiji asked hurriedly.

'Yes, let me explain. After getting bitten, the venom will enter Subbu's body through his veins and will then merge with his blood vessels, rendering Subbu paralysed. During this time, each syllable of the mantra will start revealing itself on his forehead, which will be duly noted and written by one of my assistants carefully. This is going to happen for sure because the syllables are keen on getting extracted. Once all this is done, the venom will also be extracted by the sarpas and we will have Subbu back completely,' Tantrayya explained in a deep, calming voice.

'What do you mean by saying that I will be "back"? Also, what will happen to the serpent and the sarpas, I mean the caterpillars?' I asked, with slight desperation.

'Let me explain, Subbu,' said Tantrayya. 'After getting bitten by the king cobra, your body will go into a state of paralysis. What I mean is, you will be able to move your eyes, and especially your pupils, but except for that, every other part of your body will be completely numb. Therefore, to have you back means to enable your body to recover totally from the effects of the snake bite. You will need two full days to completely recover, especially your blood cells and muscle movements. With regard to the king cobra, as I said earlier, she is my pet and so, the moment she bites you and injects venom into your body, she will come towards me and enter her nest. And you asked about the caterpillars. Well! Unfortunately, those caterpillars who will get inside your body to extract the venom will come out and within a few minutes, will succumb to their deaths. The rest of them will return to their box. Just remember one important thing, Subbu—through the entire process, try to stay as calm as possible. Try doing *pranayama* and *japa* as these things will maintain your blood pressure and reduce unwanted anxieties. I know this part will be tough for you, but still, try your best to develop a sense of quiet within your mind and body.'

The manner in which Tantrayya explained everything was enough to subdue all my latent fears, but I still had one question and was unsure whether to ask it or not. Just then, as though Swamiji had read my mind, which he easily could, he looked towards me affectionately and said, 'Subbu, just feel free to pose your question or else you will carry it through the extraction process.'

Without wasting a second, I posed my question to Tantrayya, 'I sincerely thank you for sharing all this information and I feel genuinely confident of going through the process. But I just have one more question. How painful will the cobra bite be?'

'I knew you would ask this sooner or later and my answer is the bite *will* be painful, but you will not feel a thing thanks to the queen of the sarpa caterpillars known as *Sarpashringar*. Just like the bees have their queen, these sarpa caterpillars also have theirs. My assistants have named this one Ghunghayee, which means good-looking and that is because she is stunning to look at, as if someone has applied make-up to her face! She is right here with us but she seems reluctant to show herself. I guess you will see her at the time of the extraction.'

'Oh! Is that so? But what will it actually do to not make me feel the pain?' I asked Tantrayya with fearful excitement.

'This queen will be your anaesthetist,' he replied. 'Before the king cobra bites you, we will release Ghunghayee towards you. She will simply apply her saliva-type body fluid over your forehead and this will create a numbness through your entire body. This will therefore restrict all your pain sensations and help you feel absolutely no pain. Are you satisfied?'

'Not only am I satisfied but deeply intrigued by all that you have told me. It sounds surreal. But I truly believe you, and I have decided to go ahead with all the three extractions!' I told Tantrayya.

Hearing this, Tantrayya looked towards Swamiji anticipating some response from him. Swamiji's eyes were closed but it seemed that he had heard everything. There was a long pause and then Swamiji responded. 'Subbu! After listening to Tantrayya regarding the extraction process, I am convinced that you will be all right. I have heard your decision and you have made the right one. Having said that, if you still need more time to re-think things, you are free to do so. And Tantrayya, I wish to know about the next course of action in the event that Subbu says yes.'

I was very happy about this and replied, 'Swamiji, honestly, I don't see any reason for waiting for another day to decide. You are there for me and Tantrayya has also convinced me thoroughly, which is why I am not only ready but deeply enthused to participate in all the three extractions.'

# 6

# Sharing the Plans

It was almost 2 a.m. and most of us were unable to keep our eyes open. Surprisingly, Swamiji was as fresh as he was in the morning. 'Looks like we are done for now. Let us catch up tomorrow morning for breakfast. I must leave as I have a puja starting at 3 a.m.,' said Swamiji. He got up and after respectfully acknowledging Tantrayya and his assistants, walked towards his room. We too left for our rooms to get some rest.

I could not sleep at all, although I was trying my best, due to the fact that I was thinking about everything that Tantrayya had shared. I was keen to know more, especially about the plan regarding all the three extractions.

'Wake up, wake up! It's already 8 a.m.!'

It was one of the temple cooks who also made
a special tea for me. I could not believe that it was
8 a.m. I had not even realized when I had fallen asleep.
I had totally forgotten to set the alarm on my watch.
I quickly had a shower and rushed to the same place
we had met the previous night, just outside the temple.
To my shock, no one was there. Just as I was about
to go to Swamiji's room thinking all of them could be
there, I heard someone calling my name. I looked in
that direction and noticed Tantrayya, and beside him
Swamiji. They were walking around the temple lake.

'Subbu! Please come here. We're all waiting for
you,' Tantrayya shouted out.

Without wasting a second, I ran towards them.

'Come, Subbu. First and foremost, have you had
your breakfast? If not, there are fruits waiting for
you.'

'Swamiji, I had tea and some biscuits but would
love some delicious fruits,' I smilingly told Swamiji.

He pulled out an apple from his *jholi* (woollen
bag) and offered it to me. 'An apple a day will keep
all your fears and worries away,' Swamiji said and
smiled. 'Subbu, we are here to know from Tantrayya
the way forward as regards the extraction of all the
three mantras and later the transference. Why don't
you tell us your plans, Tantrayya?'

'Swamiji, let me elucidate. I shall begin by sharing
the plans for extracting the first mantra after which
I will take you and Subbu through the third one.

Regarding the second mantra extraction, I explained almost everything to you and Subbu yesterday. Now, about the process to extract the first mantra, we will be going to Jatadhraya temple, which is located in the village of Paranahalli. This is a Shiva temple and arguably the most ancient temple of Mahadev in the world. However, the ancientness of this temple is not the main reason for conducting the extraction there. For the first extraction to be effective, we need five Aghori sadhus to conduct a *havan* (ritual) and these sadhus need to feel Shiva's energies. Actually, these Aghori sadhus normally don't visit any temples, but have agreed to come to this one. In fact, all of them recommended this temple because, according to them, this is the only temple that will enable them to conduct the havan. Fortunately for Subbu, there is truly nothing to get worried about or harbour any fear, especially because these Aghori sadhus are going to be there and will be protection for him.'

I found these words very comforting.

'Tantrayya, why will the Aghori sadhus be required, specifically? Will they be there mainly to act as protection or for more than that?'

This query from Swamiji surprised Tantrayya a bit. He smiled and replied, 'I am glad you asked me this question. For the first extraction, the mantra will be revealed through the movement of the flames emanating from the fire pit. Neither I nor my assistants have the knowledge or expertise to decipher the revelation of the mantra from the flames, but these sadhus do. Swamiji, I know that you have this knowledge but since you will be part of the transference, only a third person can do this, and so we decided to invite the Aghori sadhus and get them involved in this process.

'Also, the temple is most ancient and is actually located within the dense forest of Shangruliya. We have been told that certain areas inside this temple have very vicious energies residing in them. These energies could obstruct our extraction process and they would do this for their unexplained pleasures. But this will surely not happen because if there is one thing that these negative spirits are extremely afraid of it is the sight and presence of the Aghori sadhu, and we will have not one but five Aghori sadhus participating. So, Subbu, I reiterate that there is really nothing for you to worry about.'

'Tantrayya, I am satisfied with everything that you have explained to Subbu and me,' said Swamiji. 'Are you okay with this, Subbu? Can we give Tantrayya the green signal to go ahead with the road map for the first mantra extraction?'

'Yes, Swamiji,' I replied, joy written all over my face. I was very happy and this was especially because we were going to encounter some energies and spirits. I had truly no reason to get nervous or scared because my guru and five Aghori sadhus were going to be there. Rather than scared, I was getting extremely eager.

'Can you please tell us about the third mantra extraction and when we can initiate all the three processes?' Swamiji asked Tantrayya.

'Yes, Swamiji, let me explain and I will also share the timeline for all of them. The third mantra extraction will be done at the Alvekoondi beach and we will need only Subbu, you and myself. We will not even need my assistants. What we will need are starfish, which my team will organize. As for the process, Subbu needs to chant a few syllables that are quite easy and you will need to perform the Shiva puja on the beach. This is because it will be the final extraction and the puja will be the proclamation of the initiation of the transference of these mantras into you.

'Subbu, the final mantra extraction is the *Daridra Dukh Dahana Shiva stotram* and the process involves you chanting this Sanskrit stotram. We will repeat the chants after you.'

'That is wonderful, especially because this particular stotram is Subbu's favourite, but will it be okay for me to do the repetitions?' Swamiji asked, sneaking out a little smile.

'Yes, Swamiji! It will be a blessing to have you chant this powerful stotram. Instead of hampering the process, your recitation will, in fact, add tremendous impact. To conclude, I will now share the venue and timeline for all the processes. Today is a Friday and I suggest that we have the initiation and completion of the first extraction on the day of the Devi which would be this coming Tuesday. Activities related to the mantra extraction for all three will commence from 9 p.m. The location of the third extraction, as I had earlier mentioned, will be at Alvekoondi beach. And the location for the second mantra extraction will be in the Dhoomraketu temple inside the Bhatikala forest. The good part about the Upasani lake is that it is completely dried up, which will ensure our safety.'

# 7

# Is That Scorpion Following Me?

Tantrayya continued, 'Swamiji, we will need two days to get all the ingredients ready for these extractions and my assistants are already on it. Having said that, we will have to leave either a day before Tuesday or early Tuesday morning. You can let me know about this today or tomorrow. Travel from here to the forests of Shangruliya will take seven hours, but the final leg of the journey to the temple will be a steep ghat.'

'Tantrayya, if that is so, then let's leave a day before so that we will not be in any sort of hurry or anxiety. And Subbu will get the entire night and the first half of Tuesday to satisfy his curiosity,' said Swamiji, and he and Tantrayya had a hearty laugh.

'Swamiji, can we start working on the preparations?'

'It is a yes from my side, but you should ask Subbu.'

'Subbu, are you ready for this? And if you have any suggestions, please free to speak,' Tantrayya said to me.

'Swamiji and Tantrayya, I am more than excited about this. My curiosity has already started jumping around,' I replied with a mischievous smile.

'I need to complete my walk and I also have to get things ready for the night puja. Please feel free to continue but I will take your leave,' Swamiji said. He left for his walk and Tantrayya, his assistants and I continued to talk.

Tantrayya first introduced his assistants to me. 'Subbu, meet Sugandhim and Sanjayya. They are my assistants and my juniors. I have brought them here because both are adept at certain pujas and Sanskrit recitations which are part of the extraction processes. But the real reason they are here with me is because they are extremely hard-working and are ardent devotees of our beloved Swamiji. They wanted to help me in some way and therefore I asked them to help Swamiji in the extraction and transference process of the three mantras. Yet, there is one thing you could share with them and that is how to be curious in almost everything!'

One of the assistants spoke up, 'Namaskaram Subbu, my name is Sanjayya but you may call me Sanju, as that is how all of my temple friends address me. I have heard a lot about you and your journey of adventures with the great and revered Mahaghori sadhus. Both Suga and I are very excited to know about them and much more from you.'

'I will be greatly honoured to do so but I would be obliged if you and Sugandhim could wait until this entire thing gets over. Right now, I am excited and at the same time, filled with pleasant nervousness. Although I am a very curious person, I have never been bitten even by an ant, let alone a snake, and that too a king cobra!'

'Subbu, we are all there for you and I promise you that Tantrayya, Suga and I will make sure that nothing happens to you. The sarpa queen will ensure that you will not feel a thing through the entire snake–biting process,' said Sanju.

As Sanju was talking, I noticed something crawling towards me. At first, I assumed it to be the queen caterpillar, as the creature was almost half a foot in length, but I was wrong. As it started coming near, I realized it was a large, fierce-looking scorpion. I screamed in shock quite spontaneously.

The moment that happened, the scorpion stopped in its path and raised its hairy looking tail.

'Subbu, please remain still. It is a venomous one so don't move,' Tantrayya whispered to me.

'I am completely still or probably frozen,' I exclaimed with a nervous smile.

Cautiously, Tantrayya came forward and held the scorpion by its tail. He then stood up, walked towards the temple garden and gently placed the scorpion in the grass. After staying there for a few seconds and watching the creature crawl into the dense bushes, he returned to the place where we were seated and said, 'I think it came towards us for the warmth, but I still wonder why it was coming to you, Subbu. I have this strong feeling that the scorpion most likely knows you and has been following you for a long time.'

Saying this, he started laughing and was joined by Suga and Sanju.

# 8

# Swamiji's Puja and the Importance of Mantra Japa

After chatting casually for another hour, we decided to disperse. Sanju and Suga—as Sugandhim earnestly suggested I call him—left for their rooms. Tantrayya and I decided to take a short stroll around the temple lake.

'Subbu, my brother and friend Tadamba told me nearly everything about you and especially the various adventures and encounters you had. I know that you miss him but you have his twin brother with you now and you can be totally assured that together we will have more interesting encounters,' Tantrayya said.

'Tantrayya, I am elated that I will have you with me through all the three mantra extractions. Although we have just met, I feel deeply connected to you;

probably also due to the fact that you are Tadamba's twin brother and look exactly like him. And, at times, even your mannerisms are just like his. I do hope and pray that I get to meet him sooner rather than later. I thought he would have joined us for one of the mantra extractions at least.'

There was an elongated pause and I saw Tantrayya closing his eyes. After about a minute, he opened them. 'Subbu, I have just prayed earnestly for your wish to come true. Unfortunately, even the Aghori sadhus coming to participate in the first mantra extraction are from a different sect. But I will let Tadamba know about your keenness to see and meet him. I am one hundred per cent sure that both of you will meet in the coming future.' Tantrayya raised his head high towards the sky and exclaimed, '*Aulaakh Niranjan*!'

To be honest, just as he exclaimed this, I felt a tingling vibration all through my spine and it was deeply exhilarating.

'Subbu, I need to go to my room in order to do the planning and preparation for the first extraction. I wish to learn the *Daridra Dukh Dahana Shiva* stotram and I want you to teach it to me. I know you recite it wonderfully! Please promise me that you will teach me this stotram once we are done with all the extractions.'

I was overjoyed. 'Tantrayya, to teach you will be a divine blessing from Swamiji and my excitement towards being part of these three extractions has increased tremendously, especially knowing that you are the main person facilitating them along with your two colleagues,' I said, and prostrated myself before him. He lifted me up and hugged me affectionately.

It was almost time for the evening *aarti* (ritual) followed by my guru's night puja, which I was so keenly awaiting. Just to watch Swamiji perform the Shiv-pujan as well as the Devi-pujan had been life-altering for me and would help me dive into spiritual contemplation. As I walked towards my room to get ready, I could not stop thinking about the encounter we'd had with the scorpion. I had been coming to the Math for many years, but this was the first time I had seen a scorpion and what bewildered me all the more was the fact that it had come towards me. Something like this had never happened before.

I knew I had to ask Swamiji about it but vowed that I would ask this only after we were done with the extraction and transference of the three mantras, as I did not want to create any distraction for myself.

The next two days at the temple were peaceful and joyous. Swamiji even conducted a lecture for all the devotees there, on the topic of Mantra Japa. He explained that despite all that we are doing spiritually, what would come first was the impact and effect of chanting the mantra. Swamiji highlighted the importance and significance of the japa initiated by one's guru. What was truly amazing was the manner in which he demonstrated pranayama and sitting postures that could help a *sadhaka* or student of japa to continue their mantra chanting for a longer duration. Swamiji also emphasized the role of the erectness of the spinal cord while not only doing the mantra repetition but also while meditating.

As he was explaining and demonstrating all of this, I noticed Tantrayya seated in the last row, listening in rapt attention.

To see an expert of tantra and surely an advanced spiritual entity like Tantrayya listening to my guru with such focus was not only very touching but extremely inspiring. In fact, I was a little taken aback to see Tantrayya writing notes as Swamiji was talking. I felt a bit embarrassed and made a decision that, in future, for all my guru's lectures, I would keep a pen and writing pad with me!

# 9

# Getting Ready for the First Extraction

Finally, the day for the first extraction arrived. I was up by 4 a.m., ready for my meditation and Mantra Japa. I had been initiated by Swamiji at least nineteen years ago but still remembered every part of that amazing interaction. I completed my japa and headed for breakfast where I saw Tantrayya and his assistants. Suddenly, I saw a small dog running around.

'Come, Subbu, join us for some tasty upma and lovely coffee,' Tantrayya said.

With a plate and a cup of coffee I walked to the table where they were seated but kept wondering about the dog. I was seeing it for the first time; first the scorpion and now a dog that I had never seen in the temple! *What is happening?* I asked myself.

'Don't worry, Subbu, her name is Drishti and she is my beloved pet. She wanted to come with me and I felt it would be nice for her to get blessed by Swamiji.'

'That is wonderful, Tantrayya, but will she be joining us on our journey?' I asked.

'Yes, Subbu, she will come with us and will be a great help to me during the extraction process. I hope you are okay with this. I am sorry I did not mention it before to Swamiji and you especially. Once Swamiji arrives, I will seek his permission for the same.'

'No need for my permission. I have already blessed Drishti. She must be still very small. May she evolve to be an ardent yogi in her next life.'

It was Swamiji's voice and when I turned around, I was astonished to see Swamiji a few yards from me. What was more surprising was that the dog was being joyfully playful with him. Although she was quite tiny, she was highly robust.

'Are we all ready to leave?' Swamiji asked with a smile.

I had been tempted to go for another round of upma but after hearing Swamiji, I dropped the idea.

'Subbu, I was only joking. It is a long drive to the temple and it is better you have your second helping. I may also have a bit along with Tantrayya and you.'

I felt my appetite getting reborn and I went for the second helping of upma, one of my favourite dishes. Breakfast was done and it was truly a divine blessing to have Swamiji eat with us as he rarely had his meals in public.

At 9 a.m., we started on our journey in two vehicles. In the first car, Swamiji, Ratnaiya, Tantrayya and I were seated along with Drishti, and in the second one, were Tantrayya's assistants and a large box which I assumed was full of the material required for the extraction. It turned out that the drivers of both vehicles were brothers and more interesting was the fact that one of them was a cook who had trained at a catering college in Mumbai.

'Subbu, we will reach in a few hours and once we settle at the cottage there, I want you to join me for a walk around the temple and inside the forest. So, try to get some sleep as I know you woke up quite early this morning. In fact, the question I want to ask you is, have you have even slept or did you keep thinking about the extraction or maybe something like the Guggoorai *bhoot* (ghost)?'

'I slept a few hours last night but it is also true that, more than anything else, I am now really keen to have an encounter with this ghost,' I replied.

'Hmm, okay. But I think it would be prudent that you take a nap so that you feel fresh and then join me for the walk. What about you, Tantrayya? Are you well rested or will you also get some sleep?'

'Swamiji, thank you for your concern. I slept very well last night. I have some extraction-related work to do which will make it easier for Sanjayya and Sugandhim to help me during the process.'

'That is good to know. If you can, send a message to your assistants as well about taking some rest as the journey is long and a bit arduous.'

'Sure, Swamiji, I will do that right away. What about you, Swamiji? You too should rest for a while.'

'I will do that after I hear Subbu snoring,' Swamiji said and both he and Tantrayya laughed out loud, and even the driver joined in. I simply kept my eyes closed and pretended nothing had happened.

Soon, I was woken up by Tantrayya. 'Subbu, we have reached our destination. You can go freshen up. That is what Swamiji has told me to tell you.'

I looked around and realized Swamiji had gone and so had the driver. 'Has Swamiji left for the walk?' I asked anxiously.

'No, Subbu, he will not leave you here and go. Swamiji is standing outside and meeting the Aghori sadhus who have been keen to seek his blessings. In a few minutes, he will freshen up and head for the walk. I feel there is something Swamiji wants to tell you without anyone else around, so he wants you to join him. It was Swamiji who told me to come here and wake you up.'

I hurriedly got out of the car and ran towards what looked like a washroom. I quickly washed up, kept my bag near the temple entrance and hurried to the place where Swamiji was.

'Come, Subbu, looks like you took my advice on having a nap quite seriously. It is good, as this will make you fresh for tomorrow's extraction process,' Swamiji said as he started walking into the forest away from the temple. He suddenly looked towards me. 'I am extremely sorry but can you get my torch, the chargeable one? It is black and is in my pouch. If you don't find it, please ask Ratnaiya and he will give it to you.'

'Sure, Swamiji,' I said and ran back. I got the torch without seeking the help of Ratnaiya.

# 10

# Where Are the Serpents?

The entrance to the forest was not too far from the temple I thought to myself, but I was wrong. I later realized that the temple itself was in this forest.

It was getting dark and Swamiji switched the torch on. 'Come, Subbu, let's go deeper as it is an exciting path.' The way Swamiji said this felt as though he had been here before. He seemed very conversant with the forest and its routes. I barely managed to keep pace with him. 'I know you are getting tired but we are not just taking a walk around the forest but going towards a waterfall that not too many people are aware of.'

'If I may ask, if this place is so secretive, then how do you know about it?' I asked, without thinking twice.

'You and your curious mind!' Swamiji said with a smile and continued. 'Just like you, there was a time when I was very curious—probably more curious than you. On one of my school treks, I decided to explore this forest and while trekking I chanced upon the waterfall. I couldn't take a dip at that time due to the large serpents swimming in the pool there. But now, I hope to take a dive and this time, you will join me.'

'But aren't there serpents in that pool?' I asked.

'Well, things have changed,' Swamiji replied with a tone of supreme conviction although I was very scared.

*What if I am bitten by these serpents and then have to get bitten by a king cobra?* I thought to myself.

'Come quickly, Subbu. You need to see this amazing waterfall and we need to take that swim.'

After around fifteen minutes, I began to hear the sound of water falling on rocks—and the sound was deafening.

Suddenly, Swamiji was not to be seen anywhere and then I heard his voice. 'Subbu, you are too slow. Come fast to the top of the rock in front of you. I am here.'

I looked upwards and there was Swamiji, gazing with adoration at the mighty waterfall. 'Please be careful and alert as there are lots of red ants and I don't want you to get bitten by them.'

These words sent a shiver down my spine and I became very nervous. I was trying to figure out the location of these ants rather than getting to the top of the rock. I seemed to have quite literally frozen in fear. I stood there motionless. Swamiji noticed this and started chanting '*Shankarashtakam*' loudly. The moment this happened, I saw all the ants and there were at least a million of them. As he continued with the chanting, the ants started coming together and moving their antennae in a rhythmic manner. After doing this for a few seconds, all of them started walking back into what looked like an anthill. Just a couple of minutes passed and I could not see a single ant in the grass.

As Swamiji was chanting this stotram, he gestured to me to climb up the rock and I immediately did that. Once I was next to him, we sat there looking at the waterfall for a few more minutes.

'Subbu, I want you to get over your fear of ants and serpents as they mean no harm to anyone. The next time you find yourself in such a situation, start doing your pranayama breathing. This will calm you down and while you are doing it, try to also do your Mantra Japa as it has powerful sound vibrations. Today, you faced the ants, but tomorrow you might face more stressful and fearful situations, and I want you to be bereft of any fear. Tomorrow night is the first extraction process. Your fear could become a barrier and so, you need to be strong and brave. There are serpents in this pond even now. I will be taking a dive from the top of this rock. I am very sure none of the serpents will attack me. I would like you to join me in this pool without any fear. Look at the snakes as part of you, and when you feel the fear of encountering a serpent, think of your guru and start doing your japa. And finally, don't ever forget we were, at one point in time, serpents.'

Swamiji then took off his orange robe, walked up to the rock edge and after inhaling deeply, jumped into the pool. 'Subbu, we don't have a lot of time,' he called out from the water. 'Decide quickly. I have to be back at the temple for my night puja.'

Without overanalysing it, I took my clothes off and before I knew it, I was inside the pool. Surprisingly, the water was warm and in some places, it was quite hot as well. Swamiji was a little further away and he told me to swim towards him. I tried, but the waterfall was gushing down so heavily that I could not even balance myself. Seeing the predicament I was in, Swamiji started to swim towards me effortlessly. I was barely able to remain above the pool water and here was Swamiji, swimming without an iota of effort. *How is this possible?* I asked myself.

'It is because of breathing, especially by doing pranayama,' Swamiji said. 'Even in situations like these in the future, your japa will enhance your alertness and awareness to do the right things and make the right decisions. Subbu, your experience with the waterfall and hopefully a few words of advice will shape your future; I am supremely confident about it. Come, let us swim to the bank and walk to the temple.'

Each word of Swamiji's advice would always embed itself within my mind and this time the same happened. As he began swimming, I did the same, but this time nothing came up as resistance. I started diligently chanting my Mantra Japa. Even through the cacophony of the waterfall, I was able to listen to every syllable of the mantra and within a few minutes, I reached the shore. Swamiji was standing there waiting for me. After putting on our clothes, both of us quickly trekked to the temple. Swamiji's robe had gotten a bit wet and soiled, so he told me he would go to his room, get ready and come for the puja. 'Subbu, please meet me at this temple in ten minutes. I hope you learnt some good lessons today,' he said.

As Swamiji walked away, I was wondering about the pool, infested with water serpents. Although I had seen the ants, there was not a single snake in that waterfall-created pool. For a few seconds, I pondered on this but was also aware that I had to get ready to meet Swamiji in just about ten minutes.

# 11

# The Guggoorai Is with Us

I ran to my room which was next to Swamiji's, and saw that his room was locked from the outside. I wondered where he was and just then, someone tapped me from behind. It was Ratnaiya. 'Subbu, Swamiji has reached the temple and is waiting for you. This is a forest, so there are insects all around, especially around the electric bulbs. Therefore, Swamiji told me to give you candles instead of turning the bulbs on. Get ready soon and join us at the temple.'

I knew I had just five minutes and so I rushed inside my room.

It was the first time I was entering the washroom and I felt a bit jittery. I lit the candles and after I had a wash, I ran to the temple.

'Come, Subbu. Please join us,' Tantrayya whispered to me so as to not disturb Swamiji, who had just started preparing the flowers for the commencement of the puja. Ratnaiya lit the oil lamps and carefully placed them close to the elevated plank of wood upon which Swamiji had placed the *vigraha* (effigy) of Lord Shiva. It was almost 8 p.m. The sight of the candles all around the statue of Shiva, with the oil lamp at the centre spreading light, evoked a very different kind of excitement within me and I'm sure within Tantrayya and all the villagers who had come to participate in the puja.

More than seeing the vigraha of Shiva, my eyes were glued to my guru as he was performing the puja. I was amazed to see that Tantrayya was transfixed too. He was focused on Swamiji and his eyes were not even blinking. Even while we were repeating the Sanskrit prayers after Swamiji uttered them, Tantrayya kept his gaze set on Swamiji. His utmost reverence for my guru was deeply touching and I was finding it difficult to control my emotions. Swamiji was chanting the final Shiva prayer and when we were repeating it, I suddenly heard someone chanting something totally different. Swamiji looked in the direction from where the voice was emanating. I too was stunned because this was not a human voice! It was as if some animal was chanting. By now, Swamiji had completed the Shiva puja.

As Ratnaiya was distributing the *prasadam* (offering) to everyone, we began to hear the same voice again. I looked towards Swamiji. He was seated in the same place with his eyes closed and it looked like he was doing *anulom-vilom* pranayama. Swamiji was deeply composed and calm while many of us were shivering.

'Just remain still and start your japa and along with it, continue with pranayama breathing.' It was Swamiji and he was saying this not just to me but to everyone present there. I closed my eyes and did what Swamiji had instructed. The eerie voice that was more non-human than human was getting louder and shriller and then something unbelievable happened.

Swamiji started chanting the *Bhootaatraya* stotram at a distinctively low pitch. I had never really heard such a baritone voice coming from him ever. '*Bhootaatraya Bhoomi vayu ootassthaya. Mantra siddhaaya aarastasthe aarastasthe aarastasthe.*' Uttering these words, Swamiji spoke to that voice. 'Hey, Guggoorai! I know you are here with me. I told you at the waterfall not to scare these people. We are here for a purpose which is to conduct the extraction of the first mantra. I know this is your land and water as well as your air. On behalf of all these people, I seek your protection and blessings for this process to be completed successfully so that we can focus upon the second extraction. If you protect me and my people, especially Subbu and Tantrayya, I will consider it your divine blessing. I also wish to learn the technique to overcome death—the *mrutyu-paar-vidya*—and for this, I will interact with you tomorrow at the waterfall. I wish to thank you for your presence at the Shiva puja and your protection. The people here are not only very scared but confused, and so I urge you to return to the rock and wait for me tomorrow.'

The non-human voice began to emanate again but this time I began to hear it quite close to my face. '*Oothraam Agni Aastha. Sooksh Moksh Mantraaya.*' I heard these syllables and then there was complete silence.

I was not sure whether to open my eyes and that's when I felt a tap on my shoulder. 'Subbu, you may open your eyes. You have been brave and withstood the spirit. It was here to bless us, especially all the participants of the extraction process. Having said that, the Guggoorai was here to see you and Tantrayya. It seems to be satisfied and has returned to the rock; but rest assured, it will always be here with us. It is time for the extraction process to start. It is almost nine p.m.'

On hearing this, Tantrayya and his assistants opened their eyes and started to prepare for the process. All the other temple devotees went to have their dinner. I just sat there waiting, as I had nothing else to do.

I was finding it very difficult to stop my curious mind from wondering about all that had happened. The bhoot had been right next to me, and while I could not see it, I did hear it and feel its breath on my face. I had been so keen to see it.

Swamiji said, 'I will request it to show itself tomorrow at the waterfall. I hope you are fine with seeing it. Remember, you just have to start doing your Mantra Japa along with *Bhastrikaya* pranayama.

Having said that, your beloved guru will be standing next to you and will ensure that not a thing happens to you. I need you to be fully fit and vibrant for the remaining two extractions, especially the second one. I know you have many questions for me, including how I knew the Guggoorai ghost. I will have that interaction in Shirali with you after we have successfully completed all three extractions and the transference. I hope you can wait until then!'

'Yes, Swamiji. I will wait, but at the same time, I will keep all my questions ready, which I shall surely ask you after all this is over!'

# 12

# The Flames Dance

'Swamiji, the time of extraction has begun. The location for this is the fire pit behind the temple. Sanjayya and the Aghori sadhus dug this havan *kund*—a fire pit— for us.'

'Sure, Tantrayya. Just give me a few minutes as I need to freshen up and Subbu may have to do the same. You go ahead and be seated along with the Aghori sadhus and we will join you in exactly three minutes.'

'Okay, Swamiji. We will await your presence at the havan kund.'

Both of us went to our rooms and within a couple of minutes, we were sitting along with Tantrayya, Sanjayya, Sugandhim and the five Aghori sadhus.

Tantrayya said, 'We will begin the extraction of the first mantra from Subbu by igniting the fire inside the pit, but before this happens, all the Aghori sadhus will introduce themselves to you and Subbu.'

'*Har Har Mahadev*, Swamiji, my name is Atmabalaya. I am an Aghori sadhu from Shreekund, close to Rishikesh.'

Swamiji politely and respectfully nodded, offering his acknowledgement.

'Swamiji, I am Mrityunjalaya from the Aghori temple at Agnashini hills. I am presently pursuing an advanced course in *Yantra sadhana*,' said the second Aghori.

'*Om Namaha Shivaya*, Swamiji,' the third said. 'My name is Samadhilayaa and I belong to the Bhoomipathaya temple. I am an Aghori but also the elder brother of Atmabalaya and both of us are truly blessed to be part of this extraction process.'

'Swamiji, I am Srishti Drishti Nilayaa, addressed fondly by my friends as Srishti,' said the fourth Aghori.

After prostrating himself at the feet of Swamiji, he did the same before me as well and returned to his seat. I was a bit embarrassed at receiving a sadhu's prostration but took it in my stride. It was the turn of the fifth Aghori sadhu. The first thing that struck me was the voice. I quickly realized that this Aghori sadhu was a woman and this was extremely surprising to me as I had never met a female Aghori sadhvi in my life.

'*Pranams* (Greetings) to you, Swamiji. My name is Bhavya but my Aghori name is Sadhvi Kundali. I am the only female sadhvi in this group and probably one of the very few woman Aghoris on this planet. I feel very privileged to have your blessings and also to have been called to facilitate the extraction process.' She prostrated herself at Swamiji's feet and started making some hand gestures. She extended her right hand towards Swamiji, rotated it around the fire pit thrice and brought it back close to her abdomen. She then returned to her seat, picked up her woollen bag and pulled out a wooden container.

'Subbu, the Aghoris from the Himalayan caves have made this for you and wanted you to have it.'

'What is it?' I asked with excitement and intrigue.

'This is something that you loved while you lived with them in the caves,' she replied smilingly. The Himalayan Aghoris have sent the *lonchaeku* pickle and there is a lot of it.'

I was truly stunned at their thoughtfulness. I thanked her and after placing the wooden container beside me, I looked towards Tantrayya, signalling to him that I was ready to start the extraction process.

'Swamiji, now that all the divine Aghoris have introduced themselves, I believe we can start the extraction of the first mantra.' Swamiji nodded and Tantrayya began with a loud proclamation of '*Har Har Mahadev*'. He then told the Aghori sadhus to initiate the chanting.

Swamiji was watching the flames emanating from the havan kund and suddenly looked towards me. 'These are very rare chants which you will not hear elsewhere. These verses are from the *Agni* stotram. As you are listening, try and keep your gaze on the fire burning inside the pit and see what happens as the chanting continues.'

'Yes Swamiji,' I replied and turned towards the fire pit.

'*Oograaya beejaya sthapayae . . . oograya beejaya siddhaayae . . . Om Namaha Yadnyaaya*'—all the Aghori sadhus were chanting aloud in unison, and with passion. The manner in which they were chanting was truly spellbinding.

As I was looking towards the fire pit just as Swamiji had instructed me to do, what I saw happening in front of my eyes was unbelievable. The tiny flames that were burning inside started to vibrate vigorously and then, to my amazement, they began to steadily rise higher. I saw a lot of flames but three of them were distinct in terms of their colour. While the others were orange and red, these three were a vibrant blue, like the colour of the ocean. Within a few seconds, the blue flames jutted out and rose higher than the others to a height of more than fifteen feet. They remained there for a few seconds and then in a flash, one of the three flames rose high in the sky like a Diwali rocket and returned to the same place. However, instead of joining the other two flames, this one came towards me. I was almost numbed by this. It zoomed in to my forehead. I felt a slight burning sensation at the midpoint of my forehead but within just a couple of seconds, my entire forehead was shuddering with cold. I was not sure what was happening. I looked at Tantrayya and he told me to calm down as it was part of the mantra extraction process.

I suddenly remembered what Swamiji had told me regarding dealing with situations of stress and anxiety. I began doing my japa and along with it, I also started doing pranayama. Both kept me balanced in my body and more importantly, my mind. Then, in a second, the flame shot up towards the moonlit sky, remained there for a few seconds and returned to the fire pit, joining all the other flames. The two blue flames were still at the same place and suddenly began to dance to the chanting of the Aghori sadhus. The chanting continued and while this was happening, the two blue flames continued to form dance patterns and simultaneously retracted to where the other flames were. I must confess, the sight of the flames dancing to the Sanskrit chanting rhythm was magnificent to say the least. I looked towards Swamiji to see his reaction but his eyes were closed. He seemed to be in a state of intense meditation. Yet, as my eyes were glued to him, he raised his right hand and pointed towards the lady Aghori sadhvi.

I immediately turned towards her and saw that she was looking not just at the flames but into them and making notes in a book continuously. 'Subbu! Tap into your curious mind—can you guess what she is doing?' Swamiji asked.

I was genuinely searching for an answer but was unable to get one.

'Subbu, she is making notes of the first mantra by watching and analysing the movement of the three blue flames. They aren't dancing but are communicating each and every syllable of the mantra through different patterns—and that may look as though they are dancing.'

'Oh, is that so!' I replied.

'Yes, Subbu. I think within a few more minutes this process would be completed. If you want to peep into the book please do so, but cautiously so as not to disturb the sadhvi.'

I nodded enthusiastically and slowly leaned towards the place where she was. Due to the fire pit being quite close, enough light was emanating from the flames, making it easy for me to read her notes. I was trying my best to read and make sense of what she had written but to no avail. I saw that what she had written was neither in Hindi nor in Sanskrit, but in a language I was not aware of. The script looked very different, like they were images and not words. I sat back and decided to remain calm. I knew that either Tantrayya or Swamiji or one of the sadhus would explain it later.

# 13

# Sabotaging the Extraction

'Swamiji, the extraction is almost complete and we will initiate the transference of this mantra into you. For this, we want you to step into the fire pit.'

Hearing this, Swamiji got up from his seat, took a few steps towards the pit and addressed Tantrayya, 'How long will this process take and is there anything for Subbu to do while the transference is going on?'

'Swamiji, it will take an hour and Subbu only needs to be present. This transference will involve you sitting inside the fire pit and as the Aghoris start their chanting, the flames—especially the three blue ones—will engulf you completely. While this happens, Sadhvi Kundali will start reciting the mantra and you have to repeat it after her as loudly as possible. This recitation, with you repeating it, will happen thrice, after which you may come out of the pit. Kundali will present to you the book in which she has written the first mantra.'

'But the fire is still burning—are you saying that Swamiji will be seated inside the pit?' I asked, deeply worried.

Even as Tantrayya was about to answer me, I saw Swamiji calmly enter the pit. He then looked at Tantrayya and gestured as if to tell him not to answer me. I was wondering about this and that's when Kundali tapped me on my back. 'Don't worry about what you are seeing and about to see. Swamiji has the blessings of Agni but more than that, he has specific knowledge about the fire-embrace technique, which only some people know about. Rather than worrying, try to observe and learn like many of us are doing,' she said.

I watched as slowly and steadily the three blue flames started to grow. Within minutes, my beloved Swamiji was nowhere to be seen—he was completely engulfed by the flames. They had become humungous and I was not sure what to do. I was worried but just then, the Aghori sadhus suddenly stopped their chanting. I was seated next to them and saw that some of them were looking nervous. Just then, Tantrayya stood up and shouted, 'This is not the time or the occasion for you and your family to cause fear and obstruction in this process. Please leave or we will have to take effective measures.' He looked at all the Aghoris. 'Please continue with your chanting and do this as passionately as you were doing it before,' he told them in an assertive voice which had a strong tinge of anger.

I was not sure what was going on. The chanting continued with the same gusto but I was confused. *Who was Tantrayya speaking to or rather berating? Was it the Guggoorai spirit?* I asked myself.

The only recourse I had at that moment was to be calm and composed and not create any sort of disturbance, despite it being extremely hard to watch Swamiji engulfed by the large flames. 'Keep your eyes open and just watch like the others are doing,' I heard— and to my surprise it was none other than Swamiji's voice. I did not reply but started observing Swamiji. Although I did not know the stotram that the Aghori sadhus were chanting, I joined them by chanting the *beej aksharas*, '*Aum Ayinnnng Hreeeeng Shreeeng Gurubhyo Namaha*'. I was saying this as loud as possible with the aim of drowning out my own anxieties and worries.

My eyes were closed as I chanted other beej aksharas along with the sadhus chanting the stotram. Suddenly, someone started laughing in a shrill voice and it went on along with our chanting. After about three to four minutes, the laughter stopped. As I wondered who it was, I heard it again. It was definitely a woman's voice and an old woman's voice for sure. I was curious to find out who it was but was not willing to either open my eyes or stop the beej akshara chanting.

Through all this, I began to get the foul smell of rotting flesh. This was quite sudden and the stench was getting unbearable. Should I open my eyes or keep them shut? I was facing a scary conundrum.

'Don't worry Subbu, the spirits are trying their best to stop the transference of this mantra. They are vicious but we have Swamiji with us and so, we are all protected. Add to this, we are also protected by the Guggoorai bhoot. The transference is almost over. Please continue with your mantra chanting and concentrate on the presence of Swamiji. These vicious spirits don't stand a chance because of Swamiji.' I could tell from the voice that Tantrayya was trying to calm me.

'What is that smell? It is extremely bad and it is affecting my breathing as well as my chanting.'

'Subbu, at least four vicious spirits have been sent to stop the transference of the mantra. They are doing this to make the Aghori sadhus stop their chanting and if that happens, the entire process will get disrupted. I will not let this happen, nor will the sadhus. We will die but we will not let the process stop.'

'But what are these sprits and can I see them?' I asked Tantrayya.

'Subbu, you can surely open your eyes but whether or not you will see these demon spirits is something I will not be able to say. In any case, if you see these entities, please maintain your balance physically and composure mentally,' said Tantrayya, and walked away.

I was finding it very difficult to breathe because of the stench but this also assured me of the presence of these spirits. I slowly opened both my eyes. I looked straight at the fire pit and saw Swamiji. I was elated to see him. The flames had reduced in their size and it looked like the transference process was coming to its conclusion.

I looked around to find all five Aghori sadhus stuck to their seats continuing with their loud chanting of the stotram, which was being uttered in some language alien to me. Finally, it looked like it was all over.

# 14

# Swimming with the
# Guggoorai Bhoot

The chanting stopped and the female Aghori sadhvi, Kundali, stood up, prostrated herself before the flames and simultaneously at Swamiji and to my shock, she entered the pit while the fire was still burning. Kundali walked through the rising flames and gently placed her book at the feet of Swamiji. As this was happening, each and every person, including Tantrayya's assistants stood up and exclaimed at the highest volume, 'Har Har Mahadev' thrice to announce and in a way celebrate the completion of the first mantra extraction and transference process.

Slowly, Swamiji started walking out of the fire pit and came straight to where I was. 'Subbu, I can't thank you enough for making the extraction of the first mantra possible, which is why the transference was possible. You have displayed tremendous courage and conviction and I am extremely joyous at the manner in which you have handled yourself.'

Just then, I heard the sound of laughter in the same shrill voice. I saw a shadow literally walking away and fading into the wilderness.

'She was not alone. There were three more with her. They are extremely negative and vicious energies that people normally address as bhoot. They have gone and will not disturb any of us ever again. The process is complete and it is almost 1 a.m. I need to get back to my room and do my night puja. Tomorrow, I have a swimming session at the waterfall along with my bhoot friend.' Swamiji laughed and we walked to our rooms.

I was keen to interact with the Aghori sadhus and especially with Kundali but they too seemed tired after the long session. They also had to, along with Tantrayya and his assistants, get everything packed into the vehicles for the next day's journey back to our Math.

It was 7 by the time I woke up the next morning. I knew that it was quite late even though most of us had slept after midnight. I freshened up and came out of my room to find Tantrayya seated on the ground with his eyes closed. But the moment he heard the door to my room close, he opened his eyes. 'Good morning, Subbu! I am here to take you to the waterfall. I have packed your breakfast which you may have right now or at the rock. Swamiji reached the place an hour ago and told me to bring you there.'

'Thank you very much, Tantrayya, for all this. I am not very hungry right now and so I will have the breakfast at the waterfall along with Swamiji. I am keen to reach there sooner rather than later as we need to get back to the Math,' I responded.

Tantrayya nodded in acknowledgement and we began walking towards the waterfall, reaching the place quickly. 'This route is different and much shorter than the one Swamiji brought me through. How do you know this route, Tantrayya?' I asked with a mischievous smile.

'Subbu, there are many things and places which I have been exploring for many years. After completing my advanced level graduation in mountaineering and rappelling, I have tried to climb many mountain peaks of my beloved country. My dream, though, is to visit Mount Kailash and climb its peak. I am just waiting for permission from Mahadev.'

'I will pray to Mahadev for this to happen,' I said.

'Please do that as you are one of the very few entities on this planet who have seen him,' he said and walked away to the temple.

Swamiji was already inside the waterfall's pond, quite close to the place where the water was falling thunderously over the small rocks. 'Where have you been, you sleepy giant? Come and join us,' he said.

I quickly disrobed and dived into the pool. Fortunately, that part of the pool was quite deep, deep enough to let me swim low underwater.

'Let me also do that!' said Swamiji, and he climbed on to the rock's edge and dived into the pool. He emerged next to me and looked at the rock's edge. I was a bit intrigued by this, and then I heard a huge splash as though someone had dived into the water, but I could not see anyone or anything—just a lot of air bubbles. Before I could say anything to Swamiji, I noticed something translucent emerging out of the water and whatever it was, it was literally next to me, and I felt a bit scared.

'It is understandable that you are fearful and nervous. But there is no need for that as this is not the kind of spirit we faced last night during the mantra-transference process. This is surely a spirit but also a student of mine not only for the study of mantra sadhana but I am also teaching it how to swim,' Swamiji said. He smiled and swam away towards the deeper parts of the pool. A translucent water-shaped entity began to emerge in front of me. It was almost seven feet tall and looked like a cylindrical-shaped human being but without arms and legs. It did have something on the top that looked like a human head. But mysteriously, the 'face' was without any features, except for an eye-shaped, ball-like protrusion.

'I know we haven't met before in this life but you have been with me more than three hundred years ago as my close friend,' the entity said. 'In that life, we even studied the Aarhanyaas language of the Dakshin deities together under the tutelage of our *Parama Guru*, who is now your beloved Swamiji. I live in this forest but also visit your Shirali Math whenever I wish to learn the teachings of our guru. I am glad that I could play the role of a protector last night when those vicious demonic energies were trying to attack Swamiji and you.'

As this entity or bhoot was speaking to me, I completely lost all feelings of fear and in fact, I began to see it as my friend. The thing that intrigued me more was that it was speaking without any sort of movement in the protrusion that had seemed like a head to me.

We swam together but the Guggoorai bhoot was swimming more like a fish and using a stroke similar to the butterfly stroke and was much more agile and swift than me or even Swamiji.

I was swimming with a ghost and it was something I had never anticipated in my life!

# 15

# The Agni Vayu Beej Temple Sadhus

To be honest, more than swimming myself, I was watching the Guggoorai bhoot swim in that pool. Swamiji was practising some exercises underwater and intermittently chanting some beautiful Sanskrit stotrams. Then he said, 'Subbu, I think it is time for us to leave as we need to return to the Math and the temple for the evening puja.' He then called out to the Guggoorai bhoot and it quickly swam towards Swamiji. 'I have told Guggoorai that in the future, he needs to learn the *Daridra Dukh Dahana Shiva* stotram and he will learn it only from you since you are very good at it. Are you willing to do that?' Swamiji asked me.

'Yes Swamiji, I will teach him for sure and I hope to get to know more about Guggoorai as well,' I replied exuberantly.

Guggoorai thanked Swamiji and its image slowly faded into thin air just like it had done during our first encounter.

Swamiji and I swam for a few more minutes and then returned to the temple. A packed, piping-hot breakfast was waiting in my room.

'It is your favourite dish and it has been redone for you as the one that was there for you at the waterfall was consumed by ants and a few serpents. Have your masala dosa first and then get ready, we will commence our return journey in the next fifteen minutes.' It was Swamiji's voice from the other room. I was very touched by his loving concern for my well-being.

*How could I forget my breakfast at the waterfall!* I asked myself in anguish. There was little time to waste and so, after having my much-needed breakfast, I hurriedly got into my dry clothes and ran towards the car.

I reached it and saw there was not a single person inside. That's because everyone, including the five Aghori sadhus, was seated on the ground near the temple. Swamiji was inside performing a puja of the deity and the others were repeating the Sanskrit verses that he was chanting. Swamiji walked out indicating that the puja was complete and headed towards the car. Tantrayya and I joined Swamiji and we were off to our Shirali Math. I must say that the journey back to our Math was highly charged, mainly because of the way Tantrayya was behaving. He was profusely thanking me and Swamiji for giving him the opportunity to coordinate and facilitate the extraction and transference of the first mantra. 'I cannot express how elated I am to have successfully made this happen and I am happier that Sanjayya and Sugandhim were with me throughout the process. I am happy that with a super beginning like this we will execute the second and third processes with greater gusto and grit. We all will need these especially for the second one. Swamiji, since I am on this subject, I have a suggestion for you.'

'Sure, go ahead! I am all ears and I want Subbu also to listen attentively as the next two processes will require his utmost focus and fearlessness. Right, Subbu?' said Swamiji, looking straight at me, waiting for my reply.

'Absolutely, yes, Swamiji. I am actually looking forward to the next process and I know very well that I have truly nothing to be afraid of especially because you, my beloved guru, are there with and for me,' I said.

'Just remain strong and positive mentally and whenever you sense even a bit of apprehension or negativity within you, immediately start visualizing your guru and simultaneously start chanting your Mantra Japa, but do this mentally. Remember, mantras are most effective when uttered mentally and stotrams as well as prayers are to be done by reciting them loudly. I know I have shared these things with you and many other temple devotees but I am sharing this with you again because you are surely going to need it during both the processes. Tantrayya, please share your suggestions.'

'Yes Swamiji. After much introspection and after seeing last night's extraction process along with the transference, I genuinely believe that we should execute the third process and keep the second one as the final one. I say this because the second one is going to be a bit different compared to the first and the third, and I say this in the specific context of the extraction process in which Subbu will be deeply involved. Most importantly, I have checked with certain advanced sadhus of the Agni-Vayu-Beej temple of Kailas Parvat. I had discussed the possibility of such an interchange, and after giving it much thought, they said that there will be no issue with the change in chronology of the processes. All I need is consent from Subbu and mainly from you.'

Swamiji listened with rapt attention and then took a few deep breaths. Then, for some mysterious reason, he looked upwards as though he was telepathically speaking to someone. He then looked at me. 'What do you think, Subbu?'

'Anything is okay with me, Swamiji,' I quickly replied.

'If Subbu is fine with this, then it is a yes from me as well. And hey, I am keen to see this king cobra pet of yours and also the caterpillars and their queen.' Swamiji paused and continued, 'Tantrayya, you have done a very good job along with your assistants. More importantly though, I feel a sense of heartfelt gratitude towards the five Aghori sadhus. Will they be coming to the Math?'

'Yes, Swamiji, they were, in fact, extremely keen to visit the Shirali Math and some of the ancient temples in and around the village of Gokarna,' Tantrayya replied.

'Wonderful! I would like to meet them after the night puja, that is if they are free and do not have any other visits.'

'Swamiji, not only will they be interested but they will leave everything else just to interact with you, and the same goes for me and my assistants.'

'And the same goes with me as well!' I butted in. Hearing this, all the people in the car including the driver burst into laughter.

# 16

# Getting Primed for the Next Process

We reached the Shirali Math at approximately 7 p.m. There were separate packets of food for us there, prepared by the temple devotees. Swamiji only had fruits but I was relishing the vegetable khichdi. Ratnaiya was also having the same and as the others in the car could not finish their khichdi, the two of us had all the leftovers. We were then asked to assemble on the temple terrace where Swamiji would join us in five minutes. To my pleasant surprise, he walked in much before the five minutes had elapsed. He immediately said something to Ratnaiya, who hurriedly walked out.

'Today was a very productive day and a fantastic beginning for all of us, isn't it?' Swamiji exclaimed.

'Absolutely, and this was only because of you and your student Subbu,' Tantrayya replied and then continued. 'Swamiji, I also wish to thank my assistants and the five Aghori sadhus who played a key role especially with their collective chanting, which they did despite the disturbance from the vicious spirits. Now, I wish to let you and Subbu know about the next course of action. As I had proposed and you and Subbu accepted, we will execute the second extraction and transference process as the final one. Therefore, we should plan for and execute the third one three days from now. The location for this will be at the Alvekoondi beach on the outskirts of this village. To make the process extremely effective, it will be best if Subbu is seated beneath the waves as this will guarantee the connection to happen between Subbu and the large starfish. I believe that once they smell Subbu, they will want to explore him and will start perching themselves on his forearms. What's interesting though, is that these elusive starfish are extremely shy but probably more curious than two Subbus put together.'

'That's good to know, but I have a few questions related to this process,' said Swamiji.

'Sure, Swamiji, please ask whatever you wish. And Subbu, since you are going to be the one undergoing this process, go ahead and ask any questions or doubts.'

'Thank you,' said Swamiji. 'Before Subbu shares his queries with you, I would like to know, how long will Subbu have to be seated underneath the waves? I am a bit concerned about that. Please clarify this for me and then I shall share my other question with you.'

'I completely understand and let me explain. Through the entire extraction process, Subbu will be have to be seated completely submerged for fifteen minutes. What will make this possible is the fact that after every minute, he will be allowed to lift his head above the sea water, take a few breaths and then return underwater. This will ensure his safety. Having said that, if Subbu is able to hold his breath for seven and a half minutes continuously then that will, for sure, signify the end of that process although I know it will be extremely difficult for him to do so. I hope you are satisfied with the clarification.'

'Tantrayya, I am, but the question is, which option will Subbu choose?' Swamiji looked at me earnestly for my response.

'Swamiji, at this moment, my heart is telling me to go for the seven-and-a-half-minute option but my head is urging me to stay underwater for the full fifteen minutes. However, both my heart and head will do whatever my guru finally says,' I responded with a feeling of surrender to Swamiji.

'I have heard Subbu and I firmly believe that he is absolutely right about his head and heart. I am of the view that Subbu can go ahead with the option of staying beneath the sea water continuously for seven and a half minutes. I am aware of a certain *kriya* (feat) he has done where he had been submerged for longer than seven and a half minutes and so, I am supremely confident that he will do extremely well with the choice of staying submerged for the longer duration of time.' Swamiji's words were extremely motivational and acted like a catalyst.

'Tantrayya, I have made my decision and have chosen to go with my heart,' I said.

'Okay Subbu, but are you sure or do you still want a day to think about it?'

'Yes, Tantrayya, my confidence is completely buoyed by my guru's conviction,' I said and looked towards Swamiji who was suddenly alighting from his seat.

He leaped towards me, tapped me affectionately on my head and whispered to me, 'Subbu, not only am I sure but I am deeply confident that you will give your best during the extraction process. But I want you to practise breath-holding pranayama techniques every three hours until the time of the extraction. I feel that your ardent practice of this will ensure we are successful in the transference process. Also remember, although this process is a simpler one, please do not get complacent as we have no idea what or who may try to disrupt our efforts. I am your guru and have been and will always be there for you.' Swamiji held both my palms, chanted a prayer and then released them. Then he exclaimed, 'I am very happy that we are going through with the third process of extraction—and I am very excited about seeing the king cobra.'

# 17

# Meeting Gomtee

'My assistants are anxiously waiting to take you and Subbu to see the serpent and if you agree, Swamiji, we can do so right now,' said Tantrayya.

'Let's go ahead, Tantrayya, but please let us know if Subbu and I have to take any precautions.'

'All you both can do is try to avoid touching the serpent and also not speak to it as it has, through the years that it has been with us, developed the ability to understand Sanskrit and Hindi. There is a great possibility that you could get captivated and even hypnotized by its features, especially its eyes. To my Aghori sadhus who have assembled here, I sincerely request that you try to avoid establishing any kind of communication either with your eyes, head or your hands as this king cobra is extremely sensitive to every kind of human eye contact and human body language.'

All the Aghori sadhus nodded in acknowledgement.

Tantrayya looked to the door and using two of his fingers, he whistled thrice in a high pitch. Swamiji looked at Tantrayya and gestured with his head, asking him what he was he trying to do. There was no response from Tantrayya. Swamiji then looked at me and then towards Ratnaiya, who was absorbed in wonderment. As this was happening, the door of the terrace began to open with a creaking sound and Tantrayya's assistants walked in and whispered something in Tantrayya's ear. All three of them started discussing something among themselves animatedly. Tantrayya turned around and began walking to where Swamiji was seated.

'Swamiji, I am very sorry to say that my assistants were unable to find the king cobra. She normally doesn't leave her nest and so, I am deeply intrigued by what they have told me.'

'So, what now?' I interjected.

'Subbu, she has most likely gone into the paddy fields to satiate her hunger for rodents and more so for rat snakes, which is her favourite diet. I tried my usual whistle to call her, but there was no response. So, either I try to personally get her here or we postpone this to tomorrow.'

'Tantrayya, I will not have the time for this tomorrow due to my devi japa from tomorrow evening to the next morning, so please try now itself,' Swamiji said in a pleasantly stern voice.

'Sure, Swamiji,' said Tantrayya. He took a deep breath, started mildly beating on his throat with his fingers and then started increasing the volume of this sound. Since it was very calm and silent all around, I could hear the beating on his throat very clearly. He was doing this in a kind of a rhythm that I have never heard before. It was closest in sound to what the Amazonian tribes do, but without any rhythm or tune. All of a sudden, he stopped.

'Can you hear its hiss?' he asked me and Swamiji.

'I can't hear a thing!' I reacted. But to my surprise, I actually heard a hissing sound.

'Is it her?' I asked in a hushed voice.

'It is. I think she heard my whistle and came to me but through the back route,' Tantrayya replied.

Just then, I felt the hissing increase in volume and also in frequency.

'Subbu, for some reason, Gomtee is slithering towards you. I have no idea why this is happening. If she happens to come close to you, try your best to stay as still as possible. She may just want to explore the people here.' Within just a few seconds, I began feeling warm breath down the back of my neck and there was also this smell that I began to sense all around me.

'Subbu, please do not move even an inch because any sudden motion could trigger fear or anger in her and she could react in a way that even I am not aware of.'

There was no time for any more questions or clarifications. This serpent was over my back. I did my best to stay still and remembered what Swamiji had told me to do in situations of fear or stress: I began chanting my Mantra Japa mentally and simultaneously doing my pranayama. Strangely, within just a few seconds of deep breathing, the serpent vanished or so I thought.

'Subbu,' Tantrayya whispered to me. I could hear him, but just barely, it was that low in volume. 'Subbu, she has assessed you and now she stands tall as a token of her respect to you.'

'But, where is she and may I move? I have been completely still and I feel like stretching my arms a bit,' I said.

Tantrayya looked intensely but not at me. I noticed that he was staring at something above me. He then looked at me with a smile. 'Subbu, you may stretch your arms and after you are done, I request you to turn around as she wants to see your face. She doesn't want to come in front of you as she seems extremely shy and a bit wary as well. I have reminded her telepathically that she will be seeing you at the time of the second process of extraction but she seems keen to see you right now. Is it okay to show her your face?'

I was very confused as I was oscillating between feelings of fear and a deep sense of anticipation. This is when I closed my eyes and visualized the Mahaghori sadhus of the Himalayan mountains. This was a test and I had to pass it, I mentally asserted to myself and began to turn around.

'Do not fear when I am here,' said Swamiji, and the moment I heard him, I felt a sudden surge of fearlessness as I realized that my guru was right there with me. I turned around as Tantrayya had requested but I could see nothing, and yet I was able to hear the sound of breathing and I was sure it was the serpent.

And then it happened. I saw it, its girth was alarmingly large, almost three feet. Even before I could process this visual, I saw the serpent's face only a few feet in front of me. The lights were switched off and yet the moonlight was enough for me to see it from its face to the tip of its tail. She was massive but what was more impactful were her eyes. They seemed like the eyes of a human being.

# 18

# Gomtee's Tears

Just as Tantrayya had said, the king cobra was standing with her extremely large and broad hood upright. Although she had the typical serpent face and her fork-shaped tongue jutted out intermittently, what had me completely nonplussed were her eyes. She actually had eyes exactly like those of an adult human being and a female one at that. I was able to see them clearly, especially the retina. I was not sure whether to feel scared or stunned at this visual. To add to this and to my shock, she had eyebrows and I was left in complete amazement. Her face was glowing in the moonlight and her entire body began to shine. If someone would have asked me if I was scared, my answer would have been a big no. On the contrary, I was feeling as though the cobra was a friend of mine, just like Tadamba! I was more curious and nervous and that is when I heard Swamiji's voice again.

'She is a king cobra and highly venomous, so do not let a sense of complacency get into your mind and alter your attitude. Also, remain composed and calm with respect to your body language. I think, more then we getting to see her and especially her human eyes, she is assessing you and is aware that you will be the one participating in the extraction.'

As Swamiji was sharing all this, I felt something wet on my right wrist. This distracted me and I looked at my wrist. I was a bit bewildered to see droplets of water on it. For sure it wasn't raining. *What could this be?* I wondered to myself and quickly looked at Swamiji.

'Don't look at me, look at Gomtee as she may have the answer to your question.'

I immediately looked towards the serpent and except for her mysterious eyes, I was finding everything fuzzy and blurred. And then I rubbed my eyes in surprise when I saw that this serpent was literally shedding tears. I watched a water drop falling from one of her eyes and landing on my wrist, and when I looked up again, another tear was getting formed. As this was happening, Gomtee lowered her head and came just a few inches away from my face. There it was, her face almost touching mine; and it would be fair to say that I was completely paralysed.

I was numb mostly over my face and yet I was able to move my feet and fingers. Gomtee's eyes were close to the point where I could have plucked a few hair follicles from one of her eyebrows. Was I scared? I would say even my emotions of fear and anxiety were paralysed and that is because I was not feeling any such emotions. Rather, the only thing that was growing with each second was my curiosity. For Gomtee's eyes were hypnotic and in some way were leading me into a trance-like state. For those moments, both of us had our eyes glued to each other. I must confess her eyes were the most beautiful human eyes I had ever seen even in a human and this was a serpent. *She has eyes like a princess*, I thought to myself. Just then, I heard a whistle, just like I had a little earlier.

The moment the whistling started, Gomtee raised her head once again, swayed her hood from one side to the other and slithered away over the terrace wall in the direction of the paddy fields. By now, the whistling had stopped and there were a couple of minutes of complete silence.

I then saw Tantrayya doing the *Sheetalee* pranayama technique a few times before prostrating himself before Swamiji. He looked at me and there were tears in his eyes. 'Swamiji, I am overwhelmed with emotions of joy and that is because my Gomtee has not only shown herself, and especially her divine and enchanting eyes, but also has shed her own tears of affection and love for Subbu. I have never ever seen any serpent let alone this king cobra shed tears. They are reptilians and don't do this ever and therefore to see Gomtee do what she did makes it surreal and almost supernatural.'

'I have a question. But before that, I wish to offer my gratitude to you for bringing the king cobra and letting us see her and especially her eyes at close quarters. I, along with Subbu and all the Aghori sadhus, offer my deep respects to Gomtee,' said Swamiji. He looked towards the paddy fields and offered an intense prostration. Then he continued, 'My question, or rather a doubt, is this. Tantrayya, I have not just seen but I've even had some near-death encounters with king cobras in the jungles of Agumbe. In fact, on one occasion, I was so close to the cobra that it leapt towards me although I am sure it was only trying to scare me off. Against the backdrop of all this, I have to candidly say that your king cobra or Gomtee had very little resemblance to the anatomy of the king cobra. I have never seen a king cobra with such a massive girth. Gomtee had a girth of more than three feet and was extremely long. I estimate it to be over forty-five feet and this itself is extraordinary. Is this serpent or should I say, your Gomtee truly a king cobra and if not, then which species of snake is she?'

'Swamiji, I was sure either Subbu or you would ask me this question and I will definitely answer it.'

'Also, do explain to us about her eyes and eyebrows,' Swamiji politely interjected.

# 19

# The Mystery of Gomtee

I completely agreed with Swamiji's questions and doubts and so did all the others present on that terrace. We were waiting for Tantrayya's response with bated breath and within me, curiosity was at its bubbling best.

Tantrayya called his assistants close to him and requested them to sit down. Once they did that, he too sat next to them. He also requested all the Aghoris to come closer to him and began speaking. 'At the outset, I wish to prostrate myself before Swamiji, Subbu and my beloved Aghori sadhus as I begin with a confession. The serpent you just saw is not really the king cobra that we are familiar with. King cobras have been known to reach a maximum length of twenty feet and their girth can be no more than a maximum of half a foot, nothing more. And yet, I describe Gomtee as a king cobra, but there is a reason for this. Just like the king cobra, Gomtee makes a nest for herself as her home. She also has a similar diet. She feeds primarily on other snakes, the rat snake being her favourite meal. Just like the king cobra, Gomtee can and has even killed elephants with just one bite. What's more, she lays eggs, which eventually hatch into tiny serpents with yellow stripes. However, this is where the similarities end.

'I wish to confess that I truly am at a loss for words to say what species Gomtee belongs to. My guru, Swami Chandrayaa, quite literally chanced upon her while he was taking a swim in the Bhoohaargi-Neera lake at the base of Mount Kailash. He found Gomtee while she was swimming alone. She was still a baby. For some reason, my guru, rather than leaving her in the lake, brought her back with him to our monastery, and to the surprise of his guru, he took excellent care of her. "Why are you taking care of a serpent and by the look of it, this serpent seems to be a baby king cobra." To this question from his guru, he had no answer. He had specially made an artificial well for her because, although she would be comfortable on land, she was at home beneath the water. As she began to grow, she started eating not only other snakes but would also devour large quantities of fish, the catfish being her favourite. Even now, although her main diet is snakes, she still loves to prey on the catfish not only in lakes but in the oceans as well.

'After my guru passed through *swayamam samadhi kriya* a few years ago, two of my assistants and I have been taking care of this serpent whom we affectionately address as Gomtee. At times, she is also called Sundari, mainly because of her beautiful human eyes. I know you and especially Subbu are wondering about the eyes of a human being on a snake's face. Frankly, I too had wondered about this. Initially, her face was almost the same as that of the king cobra, but as she began growing, many of us at the monastery started noticing that her eyes were evolving into the eyes of a human, more specifically like those of a woman. To say that I was aghast at this change would be incorrect. To the contrary, I have to admit that I was pleasantly bewildered and at the same time, very excited to see human-like eyebrows as well. What's remarkable is that there was and is one aspect that we noticed when she grew to her full size.

'While she was out in the ocean and most probably trying to hunt for her food, a man approached me. He introduced himself as a tantra and *yantra kriya* specialist from Rakiraki in Fiji. "I am happy to have met you," I told him, "but what brings you here to this small temple-village?" "You are Tantrayya and I have been keen to meet you, but keener to meet the serpent you have with you. I am not here to take her away as she is your pet and I can see that she feels at home here. But there is something about this serpent that you aren't aware of. Your guru found it as a baby and she was freely swimming beneath the ocean. All of you thought it was a king cobra as these serpents also swim in lakes and rivers, and there are many other commonalities such as making nests and eating other snakes as their diet. However, the serpent you call the king cobra is completely different and I have come here to enlighten you about it."

'Swamiji, this person stayed with us for four days and during this time, he explained to me the uniqueness of this serpent's venom. He also told me that this venom can also be used as an *ahooti* or offering while performing havan. But its special use is during various processes of extraction. He stated that this serpent would be required for something important in the near future and that I would also be playing a crucial role in that. I was a bit confused with all the information he had shared and it took me more than a week to understand it all. Yet, questions kept lingering within my mind. "If this is not a king cobra and doesn't even resemble an anaconda, then which serpent is this and are there more like her?" I wondered. I lived with this doubt for a few months till I saw the same person once again but at my brother Tadamba's cave. He recognized me immediately and asked why was I looking perturbed. That is when I expressed my doubts to him. Hearing this, he started staring at me for nearly two minutes. I was not sure what to do. He then smiled at me and began explaining. "Tantrayya, the serpent you have is not a king cobra although it looks like one. This serpent is one of the most ancient species of serpents and we call it the Hebbau Divaadu serpent. Presently, there are only seven of these and you have been blessed to have one of them. These serpents are known to be the offshoot of the Kalia Naga species. So you can imagine the timeline for yourself. The remaining six serpents are scattered and there is a tribe that used to live in the remote jungles of Indonesia that looks after them wherever the serpent is. I am one of the tribesmen and so I came to meet you on the previous occasion to ascertain the well-being of the Hebbau and its caregiver, which is you. And, by the way, this particular serpent is blessed with eyes that resemble those of a human being. Even its eyebrows are like human eyebrows. I was told by one of the elders of the tribe that the eyes of the Hebbau were like humans and it also had lips like us. With time and evolution, the lips vanished to give way to the forked tongue and fangs. But the eyes probably will remain as they are now. He also told me that the Hebbau are excellent at picking up human language if properly trained. Tantrayya, I wish that you give her a pet name and address her by that name as these serpents like it. Also, you can develop a communication language with her and that way, you will be able to tell her whatever you wish her to do, especially while you are training her."

'Swamiji, I once again submit to you and all the others seated here that this serpent is not a king cobra but a Hebbau and is arguably the rarest serpent you may have seen. I am not sure if I have clarified your doubts or answered your questions accurately, but I have been very honest and shared everything there is to know about Gomtee with all of you.'

'Tantrayya, I am satisfied and keen to see her again, and I know it will happen during the second extraction and transference process. Now, I feel we should get going with the third process sooner rather than later. These are my thoughts and I leave it to Subbu and the other sadhus to share their response.' Swamiji looked at me with anxiousness on his face. He similarly looked towards the five Aghoris.

I spontaneously stood up and said to Tantrayya, 'The information you have shared has left me in pleasant wonderment. I did feel that it was a bit different from the king cobra but you helped me and all the others seated here get tremendous clarity, and I offer my deepest gratitude to you. Saying thank you to you and your guru as well as your two esteemed assistants will be a gross understatement.' I prostrated myself before Swamiji and then Tantrayya and returned to my seat. Swamiji seemed pleased with the manner in which I had expressed myself and it was evident through his facial expression.

The female Aghori stood up and started making some hand and arm motions. While doing this, she also started making breathing sounds that were like heavy exhalations. Seeing this, Tantrayya rushed towards her and immediately placed his right palm upon her forehead.

The moment this happened, she calmed down and then, looking around at us, she started speaking in a low male voice, 'All your extractions and transferences will be blessed with success. However, that witch is still waiting to create obstacles and may even take Subbu's life force. But I will be there as a protector for you and Subbu and will help you in destroying her powers. I will be waiting beneath the waterfall and will come for both the extractions and transferences as and when you call.'

'Kundali, thank you for letting the spirit talk to us. I think we have had not just a long day, but a very long and interesting evening and it will be good if we return to our rooms,' said Swamiji.

Hearing this, we got up and everyone offered a Shiva chanting, and then walked out. Swamiji and I stayed back.

## 20

# The Starfish Can Sting as Well!

It was just Swamiji and me on the terrace. 'Are you planning to sleep?' Swamiji asked and, without waiting for my answer, continued. 'Subbu, we are planning to have the third extraction after three days although Tantrayya wanted to initiate this tomorrow. I firmly believe that you need to work on your breath-holding technique and do a lot of practice. If you are fine with this timeline, please let me know. If you are okay with tomorrow, that too is fine by me.'

'Swamiji, I completely agree with you, especially with regard to practising the breath-holding technique. Also, I will get some more time to be prepared for the onslaught of the starfish. Fortunately, they are harmless and that infuses me with tremendous excitement and courage.'

Just as I was about to continue, Swamiji intervened. 'Subbu, it is good that you brought up the topic of the unique starfish. The starfish that will perch upon your forearms are not completely harmless. Each of these starfish has tiny tentacles and they definitely pack a painful sting. But they will attack only when disturbed or when they feel threatened. The sting from just one starfish can be nine out of ten on a pain-measuring scale and there will be at least twenty of them on your arms. They are similar to the sea snakes in their demeanour. I mean, they can be extremely docile as long as they are not hungry. With regard to the starfish, I personally don't see any of them stinging you because you definitely are not a prey for them. Having said that, please avoid making any untoward movement, especially in case you start feeling breathless. I therefore suggested that you get a couple of days to practise.'

We chatted till 3 a.m. about our trip to Kailash Mansarovar and my experiences, especially some unique ones during my stay with the Mahaghori sadhus in the Himalayan caves.

'You have the blessing of Mahadev and your guru always, and I am highly elated that it was you who went and brought the three mantras for me. I am aware that the extraction processes for these mantras are a bit challenging, but it is your high levels of curiosity and courage, and above all, your emotion of complete *nishta* (loyalty) in your guru, which will help you successfully participate in the next two processes of extraction.' Swamiji's words brought tears to my eyes and made me unexpectedly emotional. He had

ite words about me to me
directly. And so, to hear Swamiji say what he said was
incredibly heart-warming.

'Swamiji, the immense respect and love I feel for
you cannot be expressed in words. I am supremely
happy to have you as my guru and will always be there
to do guru *seva* (service) any time, anywhere and in any
way possible. I shall start my practice from tomorrow
and will do it in three sessions.'

'Not from tomorrow, from today, as it is 3 a.m.
You could start right now and the next two practice
sessions could be at 11 a.m. and 6 p.m. for an hour,
respectively.'

I immediately agreed and started. I made my spinal
cord erect, took a deep breath and held it for almost
six minutes. Then, after feeling nearly out of breath, I
began to exhale.

'Open your eyes, Subbu. I want to share a few
observations with you. The manner in which you
inhaled can get better and that can happen if you can
start by exhaling the breath you already have stored
inside your lungs. I also feel strongly that you should
awaken the *Daridra Dukh Dahana Shiva* stotram by
chanting three or four verses from it. The chanting
will be useful for you in generating calming and yet
extremely inspiring vibrations in your body and, more
importantly, within your mind. This will enable you
to hold your breath for a duration even beyond ten
minutes. Before you start, let me demonstrate.'

Swamiji exhaled and then began to inhale slowly and steadily. I observed that he was doing this smoothly and may have taken almost twenty seconds just to inhale. But what happened next completely baffled me. To my utter shock, Swamiji continuously held his breath in the technique of what is known as *Kumbhaka* in Sanskrit for nearly ten minutes and continued to hold it for around half an hour.

*Is this even possible?* I thought to myself. It was more than forty minutes since Swamiji had started holding his breath and I was left simply gaping at him in disbelief. I did not know whether to remind him that I was there or to remain silent.

Just then, Swamiji began the process of exhalation and he took nearly sixty seconds to complete the process. He opened his eyes and looked at his watch.

'Subbu, I may have overshot my kumbhaka process by a few minutes. I apologize for this delay but I wish to know if you observed all the three processes of inhaling or *puraaka*, retention or kumbhaka, and exhalation or *rechaka*. If you have any doubt about anything related to the breathing techniques, feel free to ask now or you can also ask me tomorrow.'

'It's absolutely clear, Swamiji, and I would like to start right now,' I told him.

I practised the breathing technique a few times but then realized that it was nearly time for Swamiji's meditation or *mantra anushthana*. I affirmed to him that I would practise this technique as he had instructed until the day of the extraction, which was two days later. The sense of excitement and exhilaration was welling up within me as I took his leave and returned to my room.

I diligently practised the breathing technique and focused mainly on the aspect of breath-holding or retention. I reached a point where I was able to not just hold it for a duration of seven and a half minutes but even surpass it.

# 21

# The Mysterious Shiva Linga

Finally, the time of the next extraction arrived. As planned, Tantrayya, Swamiji and I travelled to Alvekoondi beach. It did not take a lot of time to reach as the beach was on the outskirts of the village we were in. Since the distance was also quite short, Swamiji consented to this plan. For this particular extraction, except for Tantrayya, the starfish, my guru and myself and of course, the Indian Ocean, no other person or entity was needed for its success. Having said that, I was excited to see that the five Aghoris had joined us. They had sought permission from Tantrayya and Swamiji.

For this particular journey, one of the temple elders had organized a mini bus so we could all travel together. We had packed prasadam from the puja that Swamiji had performed in the morning at the temple.

The temple cook had also packed some vegetable khichdi for each of us in separate packets.

I was missing my dear friend Tadamba, and the others wished he had been there to not only witness this event but also offer his blessings and motivation to me. His brother Tantrayya surely compensated for his absence, though. Most importantly, Swamiji was with me and that was more than enough for me to feel extremely courageous and determined to ensure the successful completion of this extraction.

We alighted from the mini bus and as I was walking towards the tent specially set up for Swamiji and me, I was filled with childlike excitement to see a multitude of cute little sand crabs running helter-skelter all over the beach. I enjoyed watching them as they seemed innocuous and were quite playful in their demeanour.

Inside the tent, Tantrayya requested me to wear an *angavastra* (shawl). He told me that the extraction would start after half an hour because he had to perform the *Samudra pujan* and that Swamiji was going to join him. This pujan was going to be performed nearly fifty yards inside the ocean.

'That deep?' I asked Tantrayya.

'Yes Subbu, this is not the samudra pujan that people do within the shallows of the ocean or on a boat inside the ocean. This *viraata* samudra pujan entails performing the puja while the person or people are floating and getting lashed by small and large ocean waves, and sometimes even having to deal with marine creatures. A few years ago, I was doing this pujan in the Pacific Ocean near the beaches of Fiji. Suddenly, I felt a thud on the right side of my chest. The contact was so harsh that I was thrown off balance around eight feet away from my original position.

When I looked around, I saw a fin and immediately thought it was a massive shark. On reaching the shore, one of the priests of the local temple told me that it was the tail of a large sea snake. Although I could not see anything except the fin, I was quite aghast to realize that it was a sea snake and not a shark. Fortunately, nothing of this sort will happen here as I have undertaken some relevant precautions to dispel the various large sea creatures swimming in this beautiful ocean.' He then asked me to extend my right hand. When I did that, he rubbed a white powder on my palm with both his hands and then placed what looked like a smooth textured cylindrical stone on it and chanted a *shloka* (verse).

'Subbu, what you have is the *Shiva Linga*. I brought it with me to present it to you. This is not just any Shiva Linga stone but a very special one as it belonged to the legendary Mahaghori of Kailash, Swami Hruday-Shringhar. Before he merged with the River Ganga at Gomukh, he gave it to my guru and after a few years, my guru blessed me with the same. The Shiva Linga that I have presented you is going to protect you from certain invisible entities that could be sent to disrupt the mantra extraction process. The Shiva Linga will repel their efforts and will also protect your life. Having said that, please ensure that whatever happens, you hold it firmly and see that it doesn't get washed away by the waves.' He bowed before the Shiva Linga, which was, by now, firmly in my grip, and left the tent to get ready for the viraata samudra pujan.

I noticed that Swamiji was already inside the ocean and doing some intriguing hand gestures and even a few body movements. I too started getting ready and placed the Shiva Linga along with my *japamala* (prayer beads), which Swamiji had blessed me with while initiating me into Mantra Japa. After wearing the angavastra, I walked out of the tent and sat upon the wet sands close by. I began chanting my japa and completed twenty-one malas of it. After that, I decided to intensely practise pranayama.

I was a bit taken aback to see a sand crab climbing out of the pouch in which I had delicately placed my japamala and the Shiva Linga that Tantrayya had blessed me with. *Where did this crab come from?* I wondered.

Suddenly, I saw the crab right in front of me and I was all the more astonished to realize that this was not a sand crab. In fact, it wasn't even a crab. It was a scorpion and looked identical to the one I had encountered along with Tantrayya and his assistants at the temple in our village. Even before I could fathom what this was about, I saw the scorpion walking away towards the ocean. In a few seconds, it had vanished. I believe it went into the ocean and was carried away by the sea waves. Spontaneously, I prostrated myself and continued practising my breath retention. I felt I was ready to meet the waves and complete the extraction successfully.

## 22

# Breathing beneath the Ocean

I had just completed my practice and at the same time, Swamiji and Tantrayya walked into the tent completely drenched. I thought it was because of the ocean waves but Swamiji told me that just as they were getting out of the ocean, it had started to rain quite heavily. To their utter surprise, it stopped the moment they entered the tent.

'Swamiji, I believe that just as we offer sacred water to a deity, similarly I am sure the gods and goddesses have blessed us with sacred water and in a way, have reassured us of the success of this extraction and also the transference of this mantra.'

Hearing about the rains from Swamiji made me stand up and quickly peep out to check whether there was still a bit of a drizzle. But I was astounded to see absolutely clear and pleasantly sunny skies. It felt as though the sun god had taken over from the clouds. At least that is how it felt as I looked towards the sky.

Tantrayya and Swamiji had some tea along with biscuits and after relaxing for a while, Tantrayya suggested that we get ready for the extraction process. I realized at that moment that not just Tantrayya and me but even my guru was going to be involved in the process, although I was unaware and a bit confused about his role. As far as I knew, Swamiji was going to be participating in the transference process and not the extraction just as was the case during the first mantra extraction.

I decided to go with the flow and was feeling quite happy that Swamiji was going to be with me. Within a few minutes, the three of us were wading into the ocean waves and then Tantrayya requested us to stop. 'Subbu, I will request you to walk five steps farther and deeper into the ocean. Both Swamiji and I will be here at a significant distance from the place you are going to position yourself in. I would like you to walk in and sit in the Ardha-siddhasana posture. Please be prepared for the waves to either gently or aggressively thrash against you. Despite this, you must try and remain as still as possible, especially when the starfish begin to climb and perch upon your forearms. In the event you do lose your balance and fall over or to your side, compose yourself and return to the same sitting posture. I believe Swamiji has already told you that these creatures can sting and quite viciously when they feel threatened.'

I nodded, confident that I would be able to maintain my composure and calmness. I knew that nothing would happen to me, especially knowing that Swamiji was not too far from where I was, literally. I walked the five steps and then turned around to seek Tantrayya's permission to sit. Tantrayya gestured to show his consent. Swamiji was seated next to Tantrayya and his eyes were closed. He seemed to be chanting something I presumed to be some prayer or stotram. I was now seated in the Ardha-siddhasana posture. The ocean water was comfortably warm. However, I realized that the velocity as well as the size of the ocean waves had begun to rise subtly, yet steadily. Except for my head and a bit of my shoulders, everything else was submerged beneath the waves. The water was surprisingly very clear. As I looked towards Swamiji, I noticed that he was looking at me and he gestured to close my eyes and get ready for the beginning of the extraction process. Tantrayya, who was near him, also reaffirmed the same.

Yet, something was amiss. I could see Tantrayya and his assistants; the two of them were seated near the tent. Swamiji was with Tantrayya. But I could not locate the five Aghori sadhus. I was not able to see even one of them and that got me a bit worried as they were surely with us in the bus through the entire journey.

I did not have much time to think about it as Tantrayya was keen that I submerge and hold my breath for seven and a half minutes as was planned.

I decided therefore to let go of my concern about the absence of the Aghoris and after taking a deep breath through my right nostril as Swamiji had taught me, I steadily submerged my head and shoulders beneath the sea water. I settled into my japa keeping my focus completely on the retention of my breath.

Thanks to Swamiji's suggestion that I practise this specific breathing technique thrice a day, I now found that holding my breath continuously was pleasant and absolutely non-strenuous. Within a few seconds, I felt the temperature of the water reducing to the point where it started making my entire body shiver. It was possibly a couple of minutes into my retention when I began to feel something trying to climb over my arms. It began with the left arm and then the same thing started happening to my right arm. Tantrayya had told me that under no circumstances should I open my eyes as that would create unnecessary distractions and mental deviations, which could hamper the extraction efforts and also disturb the starfish. I had my japamala and also the Shiva Linga tightly clenched in my right fist and I gripped them even harder. The ocean water was getting colder with every second and simultaneously, the chanting of my japa was also getting more intense.

By now, I felt as though a multitude of starfish had completely enveloped both my forearms. It was as if someone had wrapped a leather belt very tightly around both my forearms. It was not causing any pain but I could definitely feel the starfish. Strangely, along with the tightness, I was also feeling extremely tickled. I realized that this was happening because each tentacle of these creatures was embossing something on to my forearm. I knew that the time of retention had crossed beyond five minutes although it was just an intense hunch. I had begun to freeze and this was causing me to feel uneasy. Fortunately, I felt the starfish starting to leave and I realized this the moment the tightness began to reduce and the tickling sensation vanished. By now, I was beginning to feel a bit breathless and nervousness coupled with anxiety was beginning to set in. It was at that very moment I felt someone pulling my hair. I opened my eyes not sure whether it was the right thing to do and there was Tantrayya giving me a reassuring smile.

I almost leapt out of the water but it was my exhalation that most likely caused me to jump up with urgency and a sense of happiness.

'The first leg of the extraction is over and in a couple of minutes, you will have to go underneath the sea water once again to complete the second and final leg of this process,' said Tantrayya.

I nodded and looked across to see Swamiji swimming towards me.

'I am happy with the first leg and I know that our Subbu will perform with similar focus the final leg of the extraction,' he exclaimed. 'Subbu, I know you will successfully perform the final part but just remember that during this leg of the extraction, apart from the starfish, you may encounter a few other entities that may not be that friendly. All you will need to do though, is intensify your japa and remember that I am here for you.'

# 23

# Sheetali, the Starfish

I had little time to make sense of what Tantrayya had shared. I simply inhaled deeply, reminded myself of the fact that Swamiji was near me and started to go beneath the water. The water had become warm and was becoming warmer with the passage of time. Now, the waves had become larger and were thrashing into me with more ferocity. I was seated in my position and my retention was going steadily. I was simply practising my japa and it was making me mentally composed and cool-headed. Within a few seconds, the same thing happened as before. I felt the starfish tightening their grip over both my arms and especially my forearms.

It was just then that the water temperature suddenly dropped steeply to the point where I started to shiver. Only two or three minutes had passed and I was beginning to feel deeply apprehensive and that was when I felt someone speaking to me—but it wasn't aloud. I felt as though someone was trying to communicate with me mentally. I could literally hear the voice of a young woman. 'I am Sheetali, and along with the other starfish, I am glad to be of service to your guru and you, and in this particular way. If you wish to say something to me just express that thought in your mind and it will reach me and all the other starfish even though they are busy doing their thing on your sacred forearms.'

I was not even able to pinch myself to see if what was happening was reality. *Is someone communicating with me telepathically?* I wondered.

'Subbu, this is similar to telepathy but not exactly that. Hopefully sometime in the future, we will be able to explain the science to you, in the same manner.'

I was getting a bit tense with all that was going on. I had not expected this for sure. Thanks to the breathing practice, I was comfortably able to retain my breath. I gathered all the courage within me and spoke to her through my thoughts.

'I believe your name is Sheetali and you are one of the starfish. You are communicating with me mentally as well. Do you wish to tell me something?' I asked.

'I am Sheetali and I am in charge of ensuring that the other starfish successfully perform their tasks of getting on to your forearms to create specific imprints of the mantra without any disruption. I need to tell you that as this will go on for another four and a half minutes, there will be some negative forces that could try and disturb you and specifically your breath retention. Having said that, without revealing too much, rest assured that you are going to be well protected. Just as there are negative forces, there are also very positive forces, like some of us who will do everything possible to ensure this extraction process is completed successfully. But whatever visions may happen, please maintain your strength and try not to lose your concentration. Before connecting with you, I was interacting with your guru and he told me to tell you that he is there to see that you will stay strong.'

'Sincere thanks to you for sharing all this with me. I assure you that I will not let anything come in the way of the successful completion of this extraction,' I told her.

She thanked me and told me that she would now return to the others.

All this was happening only through the exchange of our respective thoughts. Somehow, through all this, rather than slipping into wonderment about it, I was feeling extremely reassured and protected. It was surreal to think that, for the first time in my life, I had been involved in a mental type of communication with another entity, that too a starfish. I knew that dolphins were known for communicating with humans but I was finding it impossible to believe that a starfish and I were communicating.

Three minutes were left and that's when something swam past me. With the sound it made, I impulsively opened my eyes and saw an eel-like creature. It swam at the pace of a shark. I knew I had to close my eyes come what may, but that did not happen. I was unable to control my curiosity.

To my horror, I saw that the creature swimming around me was neither an eel nor a shark but resembled a very old woman with a fish tail. What scared me to my very bones was the sight of her as she came near me. I couldn't believe that what I was seeing was its human face and as she smiled at me, I saw that instead of teeth, she had four large, sharp fangs, two at the top and two at the bottom. I was nearly giving up and was beginning to feel the tightness of the pressure building up inside my chest. I knew that all that was required was for me to hold my breath just for half a minute more, and yet it seemed like a lifetime. At that very moment, I reminded myself of Swamiji's presence not too far from where I was. I knew it was now or never and after closing my eyes, I held my breath until the end. I felt the tightness on both my forearms reduce and just like the last time, the tickling also disappeared and I knew then that the final leg of the extraction had ended.

Tantrayya pulled me out and Swamiji exclaimed, 'Har Har Mahadev' thrice and immediately swam towards me. To my surprise, Swamiji hugged me with deep affection and then placed his right palm on the centre of my chest. As he did that, he started chanting a Sanskrit stotram. Then he said, 'Well done, Subbu!

You have shown tremendous courage and I believe you were and are the right choice for this.'

'Swamiji, I don't know about the choice, but the training regarding holding my breath and the technique you told me to follow, and also the Mantra Japa you initiated me into and told me to chant came extremely handy. Swamiji, I do not know what it really was but I saw a creature with fangs that was ready to attack me. At that point, I closed my eyes and remembered you and your instructions and followed them. On doing so, the creature simply vanished and I was able to complete the extraction,' I said.

Tantrayya and Swamiji looked at each other and I noticed Swamiji gesturing to him not to say anything to me. This made me all the more curious and I decided to ask Tantrayya about it later inside the tent.

# 24

# Protection beneath the Ocean

Finally, the mantra extraction process was completed and there was the same concern lingering in my head. I wondered where all the Aghori sadhus were and this time, the thought was far more intense to the point that I began to worry.

'What is the matter, Subbu? You look a bit worried. Are you experiencing any kind of pain on your forearms or some discomfort?' Tantrayya asked me with concern.

'Not at all, Tantrayya. I can see some embossing type of thing on both my forearms and I am aware that this signifies the successful extraction of the mantra from inside me. But there is one thing troubling me and has been from the time I walked into the ocean.'

'Please ask me without any hesitation. Remember I am your friend and I also respect you for the wonderfully and positively curious person that you are,' Tantrayya said.

'Tantrayya, I have looked practically everywhere but I'm very surprised to not see any of the respected Aghori sadhus, not even one of them. I initially thought they had gone to visit Lord Vishnu's temple not far from here, but they should have been back or at least been here to witness the extraction process. I have been worried about them as these Aghoris are from the extreme north and this region is new to them. Honestly, I was expecting to draw strength from them just by being able to see them as I was getting into the extraction process,' I said earnestly.

For some reason, Tantrayya smiled, and that made me wonder what was going on, but before I could express my surprise, he intervened with a response that made the ground beneath me nearly shatter completely. 'Subbu, I am aware that you are wondering about their whereabouts and are also a bit miffed with my smile. Well, it is the right time for me to tell you that each and every Aghori sadhu and sadhvi was with you through the entire extraction process. It is just that you did not, and more realistically, could not see them and that is because all of them were far from you.'

'What do you mean? Could you please elaborate?' I asked anxiously.

'I will explain. Subbu, after understanding the threats, some of which could have even hurt you fatally, Swamiji requested that he would not be in the tent but inside the ocean along with me. It was then that all the five Aghoris expressed their earnest desire to protect you and for this they decided to be under the waters of the ocean to ensure that nothing happened to the extraction or to you. You may not be aware of this but there were at least seven or eight negative and vicious spirits, of which only one was able to get close to you. But fortunately, the only thing that saved you there was Swamiji. I am glad that you closed your eyes and continued with your chanting of the japa but it was Swamiji who actually and literally battled that spirit and threw her off. It was due to the Aghori sadhus, Swamiji, along with your courage and calmness that the extraction concluded smoothly without any problems or major disruptions.'

'Did Swamiji get hurt and what about the Aghori sadhus? Where are they now?' I was deeply anguished at the knowledge that Swamiji was involved in the extraction process in this manner and was keen to meet him. But at the same time, I was feeling extremely blessed that he was the one who not only saved me but also ensured that the process was successfully completed. It was for this reason that I truly wanted to meet him.

As we walked towards the tent, it began to rain.

'Come fast but please don't try and run. I don't want you to fall and hurt yourself.' It was Swamiji and he was calling me to the tent. As I entered, he held me and asked me if I was all right. Ratnaiya brought me a foldable chair although I was keener to sit on the floor. Swamiji insisted that I sit with him. Tantrayya was also inside and sat next to Swamiji.

'Swamiji, I really have no words to tell how blessed I feel to have you as my guru. Your presence with me while I was in the ocean gave me tremendous mental and even physical strength to successfully go through the entire process. But what touched me the most is to know that you defended me against that vicious creature. Had it not been for you, I don't think I would have survived that creature's attack. I can still visualize its scary face and I'm still wondering what it was.'

'Subbu, I managed to deter it from digging its highly venomous fangs into your body but the ones who killed it so that it will not hurt anyone else in the future were none other than the five Aghori sadhus.'

'What did they do, Swamiji?' I asked, concerned.

'Tantrayya, why don't you tell him?' said Swamiji.

'Subbu, as I mentioned to you, all the Aghori sadhus were with you beneath the ocean water. They are still there now. These are highly advanced sadhus and they can stay under the water for more than seventy hours without feeling the slightest bit of breathlessness. I know you may be wondering why are they still in the ocean and not with us since the extraction has been successfully completed. Well, that is because one of them has pursued other similar creatures and some more vicious spirits lurking in the depths of this ocean, and will return only after each one of them is killed.

And before your curiosity touches the Alvekoondi skies, that Aghori is none other than Aghori Sadhvi Kundali.'

'Alone? Are you saying that she has gone to kill them on her own? If I may ask, why haven't the other Aghoris accompanied her on this dangerous mission?'

'Subbu, if there is one person among the Aghori sadhus who knows how to defeat the creatures and spirits and kill each of them, it is only Kundali. The reason none of them are here is because the others are waiting for her to come back victorious. There is a possibility that she could get injured or extremely tired and therefore the other four Aghori sadhus are waiting for her beneath the ocean. Based on what Swamiji has told us, Kundali has decimated all of them just now and within the next fifteen minutes, she will be here with the other Aghori sadhus.'

'That is wonderful,' I responded, 'but I do have a question. How is Swamiji aware of this?'

'You will know very soon.' Pat came his reply and when I looked at him, all he did was gesture to me to calm down and relax.

# 25

# The Queen Starfish
# Wants to Meet Us

The time we were spending in the tent was getting better with every minute passing by. It was already 8 p.m. and the feeling of being on the beach under the night sky was deeply spiritual. Swamiji stood up and told Tantrayya that the time had come for Kundali and the other Aghoris to come ashore. 'She has accomplished her courageous task of decimating all the evil creatures, including the spirits, and she isn't too far from the tent. We should go near the shoreline to receive her and her colleagues.'

He walked out, with Tantrayya, myself and Ratnaiya following, towards the place from where the waves receded. It was dark all around except for the moonlight and that was illuminating the sands, making it easy for us to see the waves.

'Are the Aghoris in this part of the ocean?' I asked Tantrayya in a whisper.

'Yes and Kundali has joined them. Right now I believe they are praying to Shiva after which they will start swimming towards the shoreline. We have to wait just for a few minutes,' he said and prostrated himself before the ocean. Then, looking towards the moon, Tantrayya chanted something in Sanskrit.

Swamiji took a few steps closer to the ocean and seemed excited, as if he had seen the Aghori sadhus. Before I could join Swamiji, I heard sounds emanating from the ocean and when I looked there, I saw them. Initially, I thought these were a group of dolphins swimming towards us but as they came closer, I realized that they were the five Aghori sadhus and one of them was Kundali, the most courageous one. As they came close to the shore, Swamiji gestured to Ratnaiya who immediately pulled out a large white conch from the bag he was carrying and handed it to Swamiji.

As all the Aghori sadhus started walking out of the ocean and on to the beach, Swamiji blew the conch thrice. The reverberations from the sounds of the conch quite literally filled and travelled through every part of my body. It was as though the sound vibrations, from the manner in which Swamiji was blowing the conch, were becoming three-dimensional. By now, all the Aghoris were standing with us. Swamiji had blown the conch and blessed each one of them personally by offering them three petals of the lotus flower followed by the application of sacred ash or *bhasma*. After this was done, rather than going back inside the tent, we decided to sit on the dry sands of the beach a few yards outside the tent. Swamiji also suggested that we have our dinner back at the temple rather than eat the food that was brought along, to which we happily agreed.

We were now seated in a circle but curiously, there was only one person standing and that was Kundali.

'Is there a reason why you are not sitting with us? If you wish, we can go inside the tent,' Swamiji said to her.

'It is not that at all, Swamiji. I have something with me and I thought it better to sit only after giving it to you or Subbu.'

'Oh, if that is the case, then we are more than curious to see what you intend to give us,' Swamiji responded eagerly.

Kundali quickly plucked out something from the small cotton bag that she had tied around her waist.

Whatever it was heightened my sense of anxiousness. I got worried about where the newly gifted Shiva Linga was, only to find it still tightly gripped in my right palm. I heaved a sigh of relief and waited to find out what Kundali was carrying with her, which she wanted to give Swamiji or me.

Kundali curled her fingers, brought her palm close to Swamiji and then opened it, so that Swamiji could see it with clarity. To my surprise, he deeply prostrated himself before that thing in her palm. Then, for almost ten minutes, he just stared into Kundali's palm. As he was doing it, he also intermittently nodded his head and finally closed his eyes and said a Sanskrit prayer.

'I think she wants to meet you now,' Swamiji said, looking at me. Now it was my turn to get acquainted with what was in her palm.

Kundali walked up to where I was seated and then opened her palm. What I saw shocked me, but in a very positive way. It was a starfish and its tentacles were moving. They were iridescent and stunningly beautiful to look at. 'A starfish!? What is it doing in your palm?' I asked her spontaneously.

'Meet your new fan, Sheetali, the queen starfish. She has been very keen to meet and interact with you and here she is. I believe both of you communicated with each other while the extraction was going on. She wants to speak with you and then I will take her back to the ocean.'

I respectfully acknowledged this, and welcomed Sheetali into both my palms, and we began speaking through our thoughts!

# 26

# Getting Ready for the Final Extraction . . .

'Subbu! To say that I am glad to see you especially after the extraction would be an understatement,' said Sheetali. 'Not me alone but all the other starfish have expressed their deepest gratitude to you for successfully completing this extraction and have offered their best wishes and blessings to you for effectively completing the final one. As a token of our respect for you and especially for your love and respect for your guru as well as the courage and grit you have shown all through this extraction, we have decided to bless you with an ocean pearl. Just so that you know, this pearl is from one of the rarest oysters on this planet and therefore, along with your japamala and the Shiva Linga Tantrayya gave you, please see that you keep this pearl safe. This is a very powerful pearl and it has properties to deter negative energies. No black magic will have its effects on you if you keep this pearl with you or wear it as a locket. I also want you to know that the waters of this ocean will welcome you with open arms or rather, I must say, with open waves! Any time you wish to connect with me and my other friends, all you have to do is hold the pearl gently in your left palm and mentally utter the beej akshara *Hreen* thrice. I or someone from our clan will come to greet you. Thank you once again for performing your duty towards your guru with tremendous loyalty and sincerity. The seed of nishta you have planted within me and all the others is something I will always be indebted to you for in this and the next seven lives.'

Sheetali's gesture truly touched me. Telepathically, I promised to visit the ocean to meet her and also teach her my favourite and powerful *Daridra Dukh Dahana Shiva* stotram. She profusely thanked me, and after reminding me to take good care of the pearl, she was taken to all the Aghori sadhus with whom she seemed to be having a conversation. All the Aghoris then bowed deeply before her. Then, Kundali, after seeking permission from Swamiji and Tantrayya, walked back to the shallows of the Alvekoondi beach waters with Sheetali and placed her among the waves gently, so Sheetali could return to the deep sea.

After Kundali walked back, we returned to the temple. As we ate our dinner, we discussed the entire extraction process. After dinner, we decided to meet on the terrace of the temple to understand and finalize the strategy for the final—technically the second—extraction along with the transference plan.

'Tantrayya, what about the transference of this extraction?' asked Swamiji. 'Please share it with us as well as the roles Subbu and I need to play. I'm also keen to know whether our dear Aghori sadhus can leave or will they be required for the transference and the final extraction?'

Even before Tantrayya could reply, one of the Aghori sadhus stood up and began to speak. 'Swamiji, I am an ardent student of yours and each and every time I see you, I learn something through my observations. I say this for the other sadhus as well. We are more than keen to help make the extraction process successful and we would also like to stay and help you, Tantrayya, and especially Subbu during the final extraction and transference process. And even if there is no role for us, we still will consider ourselves extremely fortunate to just look at you and learn from your actions.'

I did not know him particularly but I felt as though he and even the others had some sort of divine connection with my guru from previous lives. Swamiji heard the Aghori sadhu's words and walked up to him and hugged him.

'There was a time when the two of us used to sit under the waterfall and climb many of the Himalayan peaks, that too without any equipment. So, how can I say no to your request? I will ensure that you and all the others get to stay here and participate not only in the transference of this mantra but also in the next and final process.' Swamiji beckoned to Ratnaiya and told him to make all the necessary arrangements for each of the Aghori sadhus.

The next day at 9 a.m., after Swamiji had completed his morning meditation and puja, we assembled on the terrace of the same building where we had first met the Hebbau serpent or Gomtee as she was affectionately called by Tantrayya and his assistants.

## 27

# Gomtee Joins Us

We were waiting for Swamiji to join us and as I was looking towards the entrance, it was not Swamiji but Gomtee the serpent that entered. She slithered in and after coming close to Tantrayya, coiled up beside him. This was the first time I had seen her during daylight and the visual of this unique serpent was surreal. I was absolutely astounded by her length of almost forty-five feet and a girth over three feet. She was a giant and looked like one despite being all coiled up. Just after Gomtee, Swamiji too entered and along with him was a tall gentleman who was wearing only a large leaf around his waist. For a moment, I found myself staring at the man quite shamelessly. Swamiji gave me a stern look, which I realized immediately was a message not to stare.

I quickly turned my gaze towards the sky as though I was analysing it. After a few seconds, I looked around and saw Tantrayya silently giggling at me. Swamiji requested the gentleman to take a seat and then sat next to him. That sage seemed more interested in the serpent than in acknowledging us. But then, I felt it was something natural that could have happened to anyone after seeing an intriguing specimen like Gomtee. Before my mind could get into curiosity mode, I quickly thought of Swamiji and started chanting my Mantra Japa mentally. At the back of my mind, the question about this new person was feverishly simmering, but I still continued with my chanting.

'Subbu, you may open your eyes and stop your chanting for now. I want all of you to meet an enlightened yogi who is even more advanced than all the Aghori sadhus put together and even more powerful than the Mahaghori. I wish to have all of you touch his feet and seek his blessings. He is the one and only Shivaghori. He resides mostly on Mount Kailash and at other times, he lives beneath Lake Mansarovar. He is the most powerful entity I have come across not only in this life but through my previous seven hundred lives. In one of my previous lives, Shivaghori and I studied together in a Tibetan monastery. Even then, he was extremely wise and sharp; something I learnt from him and brought into this life. To me, he is like my guru. I needed him to help us complete the extraction and more significantly, our next and final process of transference. There is one more thing I wish to tell you, and it's that the person seated among us, Shivaghori, is himself unaware of how old he is. However, I know his age and today, at this moment, I wish to reveal it to all of you as it is something that will be a source of inspiration.'

Then Swamiji touched Shivaghori's feet and politely instructed each one of us to do the same. It was my turn and I did a complete prostration at his feet. Seeing this, Shivaghori leaned forward, held my shoulders and lifted me up towards him. 'So you are Subbu, the one who travelled with the Aghoris and stayed with the Mahaghori sadhus in their Himalayan caves. I was seeing it all but I was unable to come and join you due to my commitments related to meditation, or anushthanas—isn't that what you call it in Sanskrit?' I nodded and he continued. 'I believe you and your guru will make a trip to my small cave at the Himalayan mountains soon.'

Saying this, he started to hiss and he did that a few times in a very rhythmic manner. He then elevated his pitch and then lowered it considerably to the point as if a male was hissing in baritone. With a gesture, Shivaghori invited me to sit next to him and I did just that. While I was seated near him, he continued hissing and I noticed Gomtee moving her head from left to right in a graceful manner.

She was doing a movement that clearly resembled the martial arts technique of Tai chi. Her head was moving ever so rhythmically to the sound of the hissing and soon I, along with the others and Swamiji, began to feel a sense of wonderment. Gomtee slowly and steadily began raising her broadening hood and it was, for me, an 'Oh my god' moment. She rose higher and I looked up towards her head. Gomtee had raised her hood to a height of more than eight feet and the sight was out of this world. Shivaghori suddenly stopped making the hissing sound, stood up and leaned towards Gomtee's face. She bent down until he was only a couple of inches away from her human-like eyes.

For more than three minutes, both Shivaghori and Gomtee were locked in eye-to-eye contact. At times, Gomtee would sway her head while still looking at Shivaghori continuously. At other times, Shivaghori would move his head forward and backward and then shake it vigorously. After some time, Shivaghori bowed down to Gomtee and to my complete shock, Gomtee did the same. She then slithered towards him and touched his feet by lowering her head. She raised her head and before going back to her place, she looked at him and immediately turned to me. For a couple of seconds, we looked at each other and I felt as though she was trying to tell me something.

'Subbu, Gomtee is telling you that she will be extremely careful during the extraction process and wants you to stay courageous and curious throughout your life,' Shivaghori told me. 'Hey Shankara, haven't you taught Subbu the serpent language yet?' he smilingly asked Swamiji.

'As he gets more curious, I will teach him the language and much more. Having said that, I am keen that you teach him a few new breathing and other techniques after the extraction and transference is completed.'

'Would you be okay if I took you to my cave and taught you some techniques?' Shivaghori asked me.

'I am ready and looking forward to this. I would love to ask you a few questions related to meditation and astral travel as well,' I replied enthusiastically.

'To these questions, why wait, let us try and interact tomorrow. I believe we have a few days to go before the final extraction and I am here with Shankara in the temple till its completion,' replied Shivaghori.

Swamiji smiled at me.

I was elated and could not wait for the next morning.

It would soon be time for the afternoon puja, so we went to our rooms. Swamiji and Shivaghori planned to go for a long trek in the forest and Ratnaiya decided to stay back and help the other priests with the puja arrangements. I saw both Swamiji and Shivaghori walk towards the forested area just outside our temple and soon disappear. 'How I wish I was with them,' I thought.

# 28

# Rakshasas and an Astral Travel Technique Session

Both Swamiji and Shivaghori returned in time for the afternoon puja. What was unusual was that, instead of Swamiji, Shivaghori performed the puja and all of us participated as devotees. After lunch and an afternoon siesta, I went to the temple cafeteria to have tea. Tantrayya and Shivaghori were already there and were involved in an animated conversation. The five Aghori sadhus were also there and were busy speaking among themselves. I found a quiet place for myself and had not one but two cups of the fragrant tea. The extra milk in the tea added to its taste and it was difficult to stop at just two cups.

That night, Swamiji invited us to the terrace and started sharing intriguing memories of his encounters with bears and snakes, and some that he had of

Shivaghori and their treks into unknown jungles in the north and even in the south of India.

He suddenly looked at Tantrayya and said, 'Tantrayya, what is the plan for the transference process for the extraction we did in the ocean? Also, please share the timeline regarding the final extraction and the subsequent transference.'

'Swamiji, the plan is to have the transference process done this Friday at 11 p.m., as it is the day of goddess Devi. It's just three days away. If you give us the go-ahead, I will start with the preparations. This particular process is extremely easy and will take only fifteen minutes. It will be best performed inside the temple and in front of the goddess's idol.'

'Tantrayya, I am fine with the day as well as the time, and I also speak for Subbu and his availability. I will complete all the pujas by evening. What about the dinner aspect?'

'To be honest, it will be most appropriate to have a diet of fruits and warm or hot milk instead of having rotis or a rice type of a meal. It would be preferable to have this diet through the entire day,' Tantrayya replied.

'Will you be okay with all of this?' Swamiji asked me.

'Sure, Swamiji. Definitely,' I replied exuberantly.

'What about the timeline for the final one?' Swamiji asked again.

'Swamiji, if Subbu and you are okay, we can have the final extraction and transference processes ten days from today. That is because I will need to personally travel to Rishikesh to acquire a few special ingredients for the *Agni Havan*. This extraction is extremely important and will also be a bit more challenging for me. I had a very positive discussion with our respected Shivaghori and he will be helping us. I sincerely thank you for inviting him.'

'Tantrayya, is it possible for us to have this eight days later rather than ten, as I may have to travel to Mumbai for a very important religious function?'

'Sure, Swamiji, we can do the final process eight days from now. I will just have to leave for Rishikesh immediately after the transference process and return two days before the final one. My assistants will be here to take care of Gomtee and, to be honest, she truly is well behaved. She will be either deep within the village lake or inside the forests so as to not scare the local people. Having said that, my assistants will be here to give her the best care. I only hope that our dear Aghori sadhus will be okay with this plan.'

Tantrayya looked towards them and they offered their acceptance.

'It looks like there is a collective consensus and it is time to take some rest. Shiv and I need to go for the jungle trek under the night sky,' Swamiji said.

We stood up and returned to our rooms. I wanted to join the forest trek but was more excited knowing that I would be getting the chance to not just meet Shivaghori the next morning but even ask questions, many of which I had been wanting to get answers for. I tried to sleep but I just couldn't. I kept turning from one side to the other and back. My excitement was getting the better of my desire to sleep. I finally pulled out a pen and a writing book from my bag and started penning down all the questions I wanted to ask Shivaghori. I fell asleep only after that.

## 29

# The Caterpillar-Eating Shivaghori

The next morning, as I was having my breakfast at the temple cafeteria, Shivaghori came up to me and asked if he could have his breakfast along with me. After that, he said he would take me to the forest pond for the question-answer session—that's what he called it with a mischievous smile.

I was a bit embarrassed to have him call it that, although all I wanted was to have my doubts cleared. I was a bit unnerved when, rather than the tasty upma breakfast, I saw that he had brought a bowl filled with what looked like brown boiled noodles. I could not help but offer a bit of the upma that I was having. 'If you wish to have more I can go and get it for you!' I said.

'Thank you, Subbu, for your offer but I have stopped having this kind of cuisine for the past seventy-five years and prefer this.' He brought his bowl forward and even suggested I eat a bit as well. When I looked inside the bowl, I got the biggest shock of my life. They were definitely not noodles—they were brown worms and were surely alive as a few of them were wriggling.

'What are those?' I asked him.

'Well, it looks like the question-and-answer session has already started!' Shivaghori started laughing heartily, causing some of the other temple devotees to give us curious looks. It was natural for them to react in that manner, especially since we were within the temple premises, even though it was the cafeteria.

'Subbu, let me just say that my eating habits are very different from yours. You love your food cooked and I love it alive.' He began laughing so loud that his laughter started echoing through the cafeteria. He noticed my subtle discomfort and laughed all the more loudly. Then, seeing that a few people were giving him dirty looks, he stopped.

'On a serious note, I was born into a tribal family and while living in the jungles of Borneo with them before I left to join the Mahaghori sect, my staple food through the entire day was a bowl of earthworms and caterpillars along with fruits such as watermelons and grapes. I have maintained the same diet although the types and taste of worms and caterpillars have changed. I find them tasty and highly nutritious. These worms are from the jungle close by and I collected them during my visit yesterday with your guru. You know that a lot of people eat fish and crabs, and I eat this. I do feel you should taste this as I'm sure you will love it.'

I did not react and continued to have the upma. I finished eating and was waiting for Shivaghori to finish too. After about five minutes, once he was done, we washed our hands and started walking towards the forest lake. That was the plan to avoid other people from joining us and unintentionally disturbing us. We trekked through the forests and after about forty minutes, we were at the edge of the lake.

Shivaghori sat at the water's edge and suggested I do the same. 'Before I let you shoot your questions at me, I would like to say a few things to you. Subbu, although you know me as Shivaghori, I have a name and that name is Sadashiv. But like a few others, you may address me as Sada. I also want you to know that although you may have a multitude of different and unique questions, I will answer only those that they allow me to answer and if you are wondering who the "they" are, they are the ancient masters of yoga-shastra, tantra, mantra and stotram from interstellar dimensions. There are some aspects that are tremendously secretive and therefore the need for their permission before I share things with you. Are you okay with this condition?' he asked.

'Yes, Sada—' I abruptly stopped as this was the first time in my life I had addressed an advanced sadhu with his proper name. I murmured an apology for it and simultaneously prostrated myself before him seeking his forgiveness.

'Hey Subbu, I understand that you aren't used to addressing an advanced sadhu or a sadhvi by their name, but you may do that with me as I am giving you the permission to do so. Apart from that, I truly believe that I am beyond names and identities. By the way, how many questions do you have, tentatively? I hope it is not an examination paper,' he said, and gave me a big smile.

'Sada, I have just four questions and I am sure it will not take too long.'

Sada nodded to express his relief and smiled again. 'Before you ask them, may I request you to get into the shallows of the lake and try standing on your right toe only?'

I was deeply puzzled by his whimsical request but I needed the answers to my questions. So I entered the lake and tried my best to stand on my toe—but I just couldn't. I tried to do this a few more times and gave up.

'Sada, I just cannot do this!' I told him helplessly.

'It is okay; I shall train you on this when you come to my Himalayan cave. I will make you not only stand on one toe but also see the moon and other planets and satellites from this universe as well as some civilizations without a telescope. I will teach you astral travel or astral projection as that is what it is called in modern times. Can you come out and join me on the banks?'

I was totally amazed at what he had just said to me because the first question on my list was about the technique of astral travel.

# 30

# The Power of Visualization for Astral Travel

Before I sat in front of Sada, I touched his feet as a mark of my respect to him. I also prostrated myself before Swamiji, looking up to the sky, manifesting the image of Swamiji and mentally seeking his blessings.

I began with my first question. 'Sada, I wish to ask you about astral travel or astral projection. I have read about it in a multitude of books and have even heard sadhus and monks talk about it. Yet, I haven't heard about it in a deeper manner. What I mean by this is, I would like to know some ways of doing astral travel. I have understood that a lot of people who may not even be spiritual have learnt this art, but for some reason refrain from revealing the techniques saying that it is extremely secretive. So, I am hoping you will share your knowledge about it.'

As I spoke, Sada came closer and touched the centre of my forehead. Looking towards the sky, he inhaled deeply and replied, 'Subbu, I have already told you that I will teach you astral travel when you and Swamiji come to my abode in the Himalayan mountains. But I shall share the process that can be used to initiate the technique of astral travel. The first and most fundamental step towards astral travel is a confluence of intense concentration and, more importantly, the power of visualization. Just like the sages and spiritual aspirants use visualization to awaken their respective Kundalini centres. Having said that, to awaken astral travel possibilities, the person must visualize it with extremely sharp and intense concentration. You must start by visualizing a strong rope tied to the ceiling. The rope must have large, strong knots at regular intervals. You should then visualize yourself deciding to rise from the place you are in and pulling yourself up. You keep rising by holding on to each of the knots. While you are visualizing this process, you will find yourself actually rising to the top to a point that you reach the ceiling and are able to see your physical body lying on the ground. This could be termed as the awakening of astral travel or astral projection. However, only very few people can actually develop the acute power of visualization and in addition, it is very difficult to enhance the levels of concentration. I hope you have got a substantial level of clarity regarding astral travel. Most people explain their experiences after they get into astral projection but very few will explain the ways to do it. I see no reason why those people should not talk about the astral travel techniques as long as it is shared with spiritual aspirants.'

I was satisfied with the answer but was getting all the more excited to try and do it sooner rather than later.

'Not so soon, Subbu,' he said, noticing my expression. 'You will need a few more guidelines related to the ways to increase your concentration and this will happen only at my place. Please ask your next question.'

'Sada, my next question is two-pronged. I would like to know more about the serpent and the other question is, is it possible for other creatures to communicate with humankind? Because I had that experience with the starfish.'

'I knew you would ask me about creatures communicating with humans and I shall answer that first. Let me start by saying that just as we humans have lived on this planet, so have other creatures, some of whom lived much before us. Let alone creatures such as animals and birds, even plants communicate and not just with each other but even with humans. It is just that we have not been able to decipher their language and therefore have resorted to hand gestures and body language. Probably you were and still are a bit nonplussed by a starfish speaking to you through its thoughts. But you need to know that certain species of fish and even whales have been known to be extremely friendly to human beings. There are so many marine shows where you can see an individual communicating with dolphins and even with alligators in ways that most humans will never comprehend. And yet, this type of communication happens. But the way the starfish spoke to you through its thoughts is truly unique for you, I'm sure. She was able to tap into your mind and the language in which you were thinking. You therefore must learn that there are highly advanced creatures who are able to use sound vibrations and sonar frequencies to communicate and that is exactly what that particular starfish must have done. Having said that, it will be practically impossible for me to get into the technical details of it—it will require a few hours which we do not have. Maybe when you visit me at my home, I will share the details with you. Just remember that although we are human beings and seem to know a lot, there are creatures and plants on this planet who have much more knowledge than us. Maybe that scorpion will tell you the same one day,' Sada said and smiled, encouraging me to ask him the next question.

# 31

# The Third Question

'Sada, I noticed that rather than getting a bit spooked at seeing the serpent, Gomtee, you were very calm and composed as though you knew her. However, what was completely baffling was the sight of you swaying and Gomtee doing exactly the same thing. This went to another level when you started hissing similar to the manner in which the king cobra does and once again, the same thing happened—the Hebbau Gomtee and you were exchanging hisses. It felt as though you and Gomtee were communicating with one another through hissing. Can you please explain this and clarify my doubts as they have been lingering in my mind since yesterday.'

Sadashiv closed his eyes and turned his face to the sky. He started twisting all his fingers and began shrugging his right, then his left shoulder quite vigorously. I was beginning to get a bit concerned but had no other option than to stay there and hope he would come back to normal and answer my questions. That's what eventually happened. He stopped his varied movements and after doing some deep breathing, he opened his eyes and began answering me.

'Subbu, what you saw was not abnormal or insane but my way of seeking permission from the ancient monks and yogis to clarify these doubts. As I said earlier, I need to get their consent on certain questions as some of the knowledge is either secretive or not meant to be shared at this point in time with you. They have given me the permission and here is my answer. I would like to say that it is absolutely true that I was swaying and simultaneously exchanging hisses with Gomtee. Let me now explain this to you in greater detail. First and foremost, Gomtee, as we address her, is not an ordinary serpent. You know she is a Hebbau and not a snake, although she may look like one. She has taken the form of a serpent but is a highly advanced and ancient energy, more ancient than the ancient sadhus and monks. She commands their utmost respect even to this date. These energies weren't and still are not keen on taking a human form but for a reason I cannot reveal right now, they decided to look like snakes, especially king cobras. Please remember, the next time you encounter the king cobra, please don't assume that it is a Hebbau. All Hebbau energies aren't cobras and all cobras are also not Hebbau.

'The only way you can be sure that the king cobra lookalike is the energy called the Hebbau is when its length is more than thirty-five feet, its girth at least three feet and most notably, it has human-like eyes. When you see all these traits, be sure that it is the Hebbau. I have revealed something that, except for myself, the ancient yogis and also your guru, no one else is aware of. Even the tribe that takes care of other Hebbau energies is not aware that these are highly advanced energies. What's fascinating is that the Hebbau are very comfortable with making humankind think that they are serpents and extremely large ones at that because most people are exceedingly scared of snakes, especially venomous cobras. The Hebbau have knowledge of the *Adrushya Drishti* technique, and therefore have the ability to become completely invisible to the human eye. This is why you will not see the Hebbau if she or he doesn't want you to see them.

'Now let me share with you about the swaying and the hissing. The Hebbau are advanced energy forms and being from beyond this planet, most of them are disguised as serpents. Due to this, they can do what other serpents do to communicate, which is the act of hissing. This is a language only a few people know, such as my three acharyas, my parama guru and a Mahaghori sadhu of the Himalayas. What will stun you is that even your Swamiji knows the serpent language but what's strange is that, except for our guru, Mahadev, none of us have the permission to teach this to anyone. What you saw that day was the Hebbau telling me about you and her excitement about participating in the extraction process. There's one more thing before you ask your next question. Just as most of these energies have taken the form of the serpent, similarly there are other energies that are more advanced and have taken other forms, including some marine creatures like the starfish,' he said and gave me a mischievous smile.

'Oh! So that starfish, Sheetali, and others on my forearm were not really starfish but advanced energies just like Gomtee!' I exclaimed.

'Subbu, you need to calm down. What you have seen until now through the Hebbau and the starfish is just the tip of the iceberg as there are a lot more around us and a few are even living among us as humans. If you have any more questions, please ask as it is getting time for the stotram recitation by Shankara, your Swamiji. He is teaching me some ancient chanting and you are coming with me, that is, if you are free.'

'I will be more than happy to join you, Sada, as these opportunities don't come often. I don't have any other work-related commitments. I just have one more question and I hope you will answer it for me.'

'Sure, I'll try my best and I hope I will have the answers and their permission to put forth my replies!' Sadashiv responded with a hopeful look on his uniquely shaped face.

I say uniquely shaped because his face was truly different. It was around a foot long and oblong in shape. In fact, when I first saw him I thought he was an alien being, but the moment I saw his entire body, I realized he was definitely a human or at least that is what I thought. He wasn't.

# 32

# Spirits and Ghosts

I took advantage of the chance to ask a few more questions. 'Sada, although I have asked others about this, I want to know your perspective on spirits and ghosts because I have had people tell me about their encounters. Even during the first extraction, Swamiji introduced me to a spirit that said it would protect us against any kind of negative spirits. I'm sure it will be there for the next extraction and transference.'

'Subbu, it will be there also during the transference of the second extraction process. You probably should have asked it about ghosts and sprits,' Sadashiv interjected.

'But I wish to know what you think,' I replied with a smile.

'Sure Subbu! Let me share a bit of my knowledge with you. Are ghosts and spirits a reality? The answer is yes. Let me start by saying that we can call them all spirits. Terms like ghosts, energies, poltergeists and others are different words that mean the same thing. It is like we are all human beings and yet there are different types of vibrations or intensities. For example, if there is a sage meditating in a cave beneath Lake Mansarovar, there will also be a gangster who is troubling people and doing the most notorious acts. Interestingly, both are humans like you and me. It is similar with such entities or energies. Having said that, the spirits exist in a dimension that we human beings or even other creatures are not allowed to enter and that is the law of life. Yet, there are and will be certain anomalies that make it possible for entities from both dimensions to either crossover or be lured or compelled to crossover.

'Certain spirits can be manipulated in some ways, especially by humans like *tantriks* or witches, to cause hurt and pain, whether mentally or physically, to others. Most of the time, such acts are done for money by a few who have studied such aspects of tantras and mantras and are shamelessly misusing the power only to get something in return. There are also certain spirits who exist in our world on their own willpower or who need to realize their unfulfilled desires. Most of them will not want to engage with humans or other kinds of beings here on earth but could become susceptible to and fall at the mercy of the tantriks or practitioners of what most of you call black magic.'

'Regarding black magic, is there any way by which I or others like me can be protected from getting affected by it?' I asked.

'In your case, there is absolutely nothing to worry about because you not only have your guru and his blessings but also the strength and protection of the Mahaghoris with whom you spent a great amount of time. There are many like you who need not worry about getting affected by black magic because of your respective gurus. There are also others who will not be affected because of certain protection-related stotrams and prayers they chant regularly. In fact, I am aware that you also chant the *Shiv Kavach*, to which you were initiated by your guru. Believe me, chanting this itself will protect you as its vibrations act as a very powerful shield. Apart from this, even the continuous chanting of the beej aksharas, namely *Aum, Aaieen, Hreen* and *Shreen*, causes extremely powerful and positive vibrations that are known to envelop the person chanting them.

'There are a few more ways to prevent black tantra magic from even getting close to us, but I have been told by them not to reveal them to you at this moment in time. Remember, there are also certain energies or spirits that are divine and always willing to help. The spirit you encountered at the forest pond during your first extraction is one of them. It used to be a good friend and a co-student of your guru and it will always be there for him and even for his students like you. To extend my perspective on this topic, let me add that there have been occasions where extremely strong and evil spirits have been known to identify and hone in on mentally weak human beings and then possess them either partially or completely. It is for this reason we all must continue chanting as well as reciting prayers, whatever your faith may be. Creating strong vibrations through chanting as well as prayers can deter the spirits from even coming close to you.

'Subbu, I have seen spirits in the form of smoky shadows and there are many in the present times who could have had such experiences. But please understand that they cannot do anything to me or people like me as long as we are intensely doing our chanting. To you also, if you see or even feel something like this, start your *Daridra Dukh Dahana Shiva* stotram or even your Shiv Kavach and while doing this, try to visualize the vibrant image of your guru. I assure you nothing will happen to you. I think I have shared a lot about spirits and ghosts. There is more but let us save that information for another time.'

'Sada, I say this with complete candidness that I have come to know more about such entities than I had ever imagined. Most of the time, people would share their experiences but not information like you have shared. I feel a sense of supreme clarity and courage as well. I truly am thankful to you.'

# 33

# Leaf Paste and Snake Venom

'Sada, my next question is a bit different and I actually do not know whether to ask you or not.'

'Subbu, you are Shankara's student and therefore you are free to ask me whatever question you wish to. I hope I will have the answer, so please go ahead.'

'Thank you so much. I wanted to know if there are plants and flowers or other things that have medicinal properties. To give you a backstory, I have seen a lot of documentaries and read things on the Internet where researchers have been shown travelling to the Amazon jungles and encountering unique plants and trees which have medicinal properties. A few of these documentaries got me thinking and therefore, I'd like to hear your thoughts about it.'

'The question you have asked regarding the medicinal aspects of plants and trees is quite profound and here is my response. I have personally been a witness to an incident in the forests of Bhoomigiri near Mangalore. This happened when I was twenty-five years old. We were on a trek to the Yamkundoo mountains within that forest. As we were walking, I heard one of our colleagues screaming on top of his voice and saying that he had been spat on by a cobra. There aren't any species of spitting cobras in India and therefore I was surprised. I was later told there is a very special species of the kudasku viper that mimics a cobra and also spits venom accurately into the eyes of its prey. It was this viper species that had attacked our colleague as he was trying to catch it with his snake tongs. What was beautifully strange was the fact that within minutes of his being spat on, one of the guides who also had deep knowledge of the forest spotted a large tree and began climbing it. He then returned with a few leaves in his hands.

'He was in a rush to make a paste of it by using his saliva as a mixing agent. It was a bit difficult to see him do this but we had no option in the dense jungle without any doctors. The venom had entered our colleague's eyes, one of which had started to bleed profusely. The leaves were made into a gooey semi-thick paste and the guide slowly and steadily poured a few drops of it directly into both eyes. Until then, our colleague was writhing in intolerable pain but within just a few moments, he significantly calmed down. To our astonishment, just after a couple of hours, he was completely all right and encouraged us to continue our trek. I was completely stunned. This was the first time I witnessed the manner in which a paste made from the leaves of a jungle tree saved my friend from turning totally blind and probably even from eventual death. The biodiversity across this planet is awesome.

'You will be impressed to know that there is a certain seaweed lying deep beneath the Pacific Ocean that has the medicinal abilities to completely cure a person of severe asthma. Some flowers that grow on the edge of this particular lake at the foothills of Mount Kailash, when had with cow milk, can cure migraines forever. I am proof of this because I was suffering from severe headaches that would make me so disoriented that at times I would bang my head to just decrease the pain. This continued for many years. But it was during my stay with my guru at the base of Mount Kailash that one of the sadhus living with us made me have the flowers with cow milk. To my surprise, in just a week of having this drink daily, my migraines just vanished and neither headaches nor migraines have ever affected me since then!

'Subbu, I can tell you for sure that even inside the pond we are sitting beside there are medicinal plants and all we have to do is dive deep and search for them. Our planet is extremely and vibrantly diverse and you know that, especially with your experiences with mushrooms and other things you encountered while you were with the Mahaghoris. Your good friend and Tantrayya's twin brother Tadamba is also my student. He is learning about the deeper and very strong Kundalini chakras that are located even above the Sahasrara chakra, something I intend to teach you hopefully in this life itself.'

# 34

# 'I Am Not Completely Human'

'Your Swamiji had warned me about your extreme levels of curiosity and I now realize how right he was,' said Sadashiv and he started laughing loudly. His way of laughing was also quite peculiar—it was like a hyena's! His laughter was quite infectious and got me laughing as well even though the joke was on me.

'Hey Subbu, please don't feel offended by all this as I am that way only. Humour and me always travel together. If you have any more questions, please ask without hesitation,' he said affectionately.

'I cannot thank you enough for responding to all my questions. I have just one final question. What I am really keen to find out is about you. Who are you? I do not mean this in terms of when and where you were born and your life story. I honestly wish to know—are you human like us or different? It is a very childish question but I do want to know this. That is because, from the time I have been introduced to you, I felt there was something non-human about you. Even the shape of your face is very different. You have no eyebrows, you have not a single strand of hair on your head and strangely, your arms are so long that they go below your knees, which to me is quite unnatural. I noticed you have just one nostril, which by itself is shaped like that of an eagle's. These features aren't what we usually see in humans. Please allow me to share a few other things that are very unusual. I observed your feet and at first glance, they look like normal human feet. But, on closer observation, I realized that your feet have three toes and maybe because of that, you walk differently as well. You have eyes identical to those of the Hebbau serpent and it was beautifully eerie to see you and the serpent looking at each other as if you have known her for a very long time. All this leaves me with my final question—who are you, really?'

After sharing all this, I felt a sense of relief, as if a load of pressure was off my back. Sadashiv looked at me sternly. It was more like a very focused stare, directly into my eyes. After a few seconds of doing that, he looked up to the sky for a few minutes. I was not sure what I was supposed to do as he would stare at me and then immediately look at the sky. Nearly five minutes passed by and I was about to say something, when he began to speak. For a moment I thought he was speaking in Kannada or Malayalam, but the more

I heard it, the more convinced I was that it was neither! I was intensely puzzled by this but then he started speaking in English.

'Subbu, the language you initially heard me speak in was Hounchak, a language not of this planet. I wanted to tell you the name of the planet but I have been strictly warned not to do so. By now you may have inferred correctly that I am not a human. Well, actually, I am not a complete human and I truly think you are not just curious but highly observant because you were very accurate in sharing the differences about me, with me. Yes Subbu, I have the human gene but along with that, I also have an alien gene within me. I have been existing with this alien gene for the past three thousand years. Please understand that the alien element does not mean that we are dangerous or that we look like alien beings from a Hollywood movie. I and some of us residing on Earth belong to a different planet, which is not even part of the Milky Way solar system. We have the human gene as well and so, we hopefully have the best of both entities. The reason why I live among the Himalayan mountains is because of our alien ancestors who used to arrive from other solar systems to Earth either at the banks of Lake Mansarovar or at the base of Mount Kailash or a few Himalayan peaks. Till today, they come to Earth and the place they land at is next to the Himalayan cave where I live. What's fascinating is that my alien ancestors have a differently shaped body which is translucent in nature. At times, there are other alien but highly spiritual beings that arrive at Lake Mansarovar to take a holy dip. For me, all these alien beings from Mount Kailash as well as Lake Mansarovar are on Earth as a matter of fact. In reality though, they are revered by people on Earth and more so from other planets and stars. I have not shared all this information with anyone except your beloved Swamiji. I trust you will keep it to yourself. I am a human when I am on this beautiful planet and an alien when I go to the other planet!'

'Sada, I cannot say that I am shocked listening to your answer and that is because I had suspected it. But I wanted to hear it from your mouth, which is also unique and different from ours. This was technically my final question and therefore, for now, I am satisfied with your replies to all my questions. I have, thanks to you, a clearer comprehension of a lot of aspects about which I was in doubt.'

I then offered a full and complete prostration at his feet. As this happened, he thanked me for helping him to refresh his own knowledge. After that, he requested me to wait for a few moments as he wanted to take a quick dip in the waters of the forest lake.

# 35

# Transference of the Extracted Mantra

It had been a few minutes since Sadashiv had dived into the lake. While he was taking his dip, I noticed an extremely large scorpion climbing the rock next to me. I was, for a moment, stunned at the sight and then decided to observe it as it posed no threat to my life. I was so engrossed in closely watching the scorpion that I did not realize Sadashiv was standing just behind me.

'If you are done with analysing the scorpion, can we return to the temple? As I mentioned earlier, there is a stotram recitation and teaching session by Shankara, your guru.'

'Yes! But I am quite sure that this is the same scorpion I have been seeing and it is making me anxious,' I said as I stood up to join him for the trek back to the temple.

Sadashiv looked at me and smiled. 'There are certain questions to which I feel only you may have to find the answers to. I can only hope that in due time you will,' he said and blessed me by tapping my forehead.

Sadashiv and I returned to the temple and were told by Ratnaiya that Swamiji had already reached the terrace and was waiting not just for Sadashiv but he also wanted me to attend the session. Both of us freshened up and ran to the terrace assuming that we were late.

As I opened the door, I saw that Swamiji was not alone. Tantrayya was there with the five Aghori sadhus and they were seated in a circle.

'*Har Har Mahadev*!' Swamiji exclaimed upon seeing me and Sadashiv, and he was in a joyous mood. 'How was the trek and, more importantly, the question-answer session? I hope Subbu did not trouble you a lot with his never-ending flow of doubts and questions,' he said and started to laugh aloud, with Sadashiv quickly joining in.

During that session, Swamiji taught us an extremely elegant and powerful stotram called *Lingashtakam*. His chant was melodious and with powerful intonations simultaneously, and he made us recite each line in a similar way. When the session was over, tea was served to us at the polite insistence of Swamiji. Except for the Aghori sadhvi, Kundali, everyone else relished the tea with a few of them even having three cups.

'Before we leave, Tantrayya, will you please tell us about the planning and execution of the transference process for the third mantra?'

'Yes, Swamiji, let me articulate the entire plan. As I mentioned, we will initiate the process day after tomorrow, which is a Friday and also the day of the Devi. The location will be the same Alvekoondi beach, but this time Swamiji will not have to be inside the ocean, although both he and Subbu will be seated on its sands, specifically the wet sands. The most effective time for the transference process to be carried out is 1 a.m. as that is when the moonlight will be at its peak and the ocean will be calm. The duration of this process will be only ten minutes and we should be back at this temple by 3 a.m. latest. All the ingredients that will be required to carry out this process successfully and avert any possible threats have already been procured by my assistants. All in all, we are ready for the transference and will await the green signal from Subbu and Swamiji.'

Sadashiv spoke up then. 'What about me? Do I also get to come and witness this process? And what about all these Aghori sadhus?' he asked in what seemed to me a slightly strange tone.

'To be very honest, this is supposed to be very private and we would prefer it if no one else attends, except for Subbu, Swamiji, myself and my assistants. However, we have requested the Aghoris to be with us as they have the wherewithal to deal with negative and vicious spirits that may relentlessly try to stop the transference process from getting executed. Most importantly, Shivaghori, I need you to be there and act as an overall protection. Frankly, it would be an honour to have you with us all through the process and also for the next one for which your presence and cooperation will be most needed.'

Tantrayya then prostrated himself before Swamiji and Sadashiv, and then we left the terrace to return to our respective chores. Swamiji was still seated and requested Sadashiv to stay back. I presumed they had something to discuss—at least that is what Ratnaiya told me as he was getting into the cafeteria.

Finally, the night of the Devi came, and everyone was ready and set to go to Alvekoondi beach. It was almost 10 p.m. when the Tempo Traveller reached the destination. Swamiji asked us to alight from the bus and then we assembled inside a tent that was larger but similar to the one we'd been in during the previous extraction process. We had some tea and then Swamiji walked out alone towards the beach. He bowed deeply to the incoming waves, sat on the beach and began chanting loudly in what sounded to me like Sanskrit. After a few minutes, he became silent and started meditating.

Sadashiv said, 'Subbu, what you heard was not Sanskrit although it sounds like it. It was our alien language. Only he knows this language as I was the one who taught it to him and we revised it on the same day we had our terrace meeting.'

# 36

# Distraction

When Swamiji returned from his meditation, Tantrayya came up to us and said, 'I think it is time get started and therefore I request Swamiji and you to sit on the wet sand, but not too far from the dry sand.'

We were able to find such a spot and it was interesting to find ourselves seated almost equidistant from the dry sands and the waves. It seemed as though it had been appropriately measured. Tantrayya and his assistants came to us and with Swamiji's permission, Tantrayya sat exactly between Swamiji and me. He told his assistants to light a fire and simultaneously begin the *Chandrakala* stotram. He requested them to chant as loudly as possible because the sound of the ocean waves was quite loud. 'It is vital that all three of us hear each and every syllable of the chanting till the completion of the transference process. And hey, also ensure that the fire doesn't get extinguished come what may.'

He then told both of us to close our eyes and just listen as intently as possible to the chanting.

The chanting immediately began and at a distance, a fire was lit. I guessed that the fire pit had been created even before we arrived and it looked like a *dhuni* (sacred site) that sadhus would sit in front of. As I was listening attentively to the chants, I also began to hear whispers. It was as though someone was speaking to me and trying to say something. I had my eyes open and could see there was no one near me. Swamiji was seated six feet away from where I was. Tantrayya too was a bit far and intensely chanting.

'If there is no one around me, then who is speaking to me?' I wondered.

'Subbu, do not pay attention to the whispers, please intensify your focus and concentration on the sound vibrations of the chanting. It is important that you listen to it all through the process. This is just the beginning,' said Swamiji, who was alerting me.

'My apologies, Swamiji, for getting distracted,' I said.

'Subbu, I am with you and will be with you through this. You have nothing to worry because, apart from your guru, the five Aghori sadhus and Sadashiv are here for your safety and mine. Having said that, there are a few things you will have to be extremely strong-willed about. More than physical harm, they will try their best to harm you as well as me mentally. For that not to happen, I want you to continuously do your mantra chanting while ensuring that you are able to listen to the chanting by Tantrayya and his assistants. I know it will be a challenge but this is where your mental strength will be tested. Subbu, it is not just you but I too have been hearing a deep voice and whatever I am telling you is what I am practising myself. I am prepared for everything that will happen from here on.'

'Swamiji, I will do everything you have told me to do. I will be as strong as I was during the first extraction and transference. Just knowing that you are there with me and guiding me whenever required is a blessing and I am thankful to you for that. Is it okay if I keep my eyes open as this process is happening?' I asked nervously.

'You can surely keep your eyes open whenever possible but remember to close them if told to do so. This process is about transference of the mantra from you, through your forearms into me and so, you can take it a bit easy.' Swamiji then closed his eyes, straightened his spine and slowly, yet steadily slipped into an intense meditative state. The chanting was going on and even the Aghori sadhus joined in. The reverberations created through this were almost supernatural. My eyes were open and I felt the atmosphere getting deeply charged. Sadashiv was seated a bit far from Swamiji and me but it looked like the chanting was having its amazing impact on him—seated on the sands, he was swaying his upper body quite vigorously and at times, he even moved his head forward and back in a very graceful manner.

Suddenly, as the chanting was going on, I heard someone laughing at an extremely high pitch. It sounded like the neighing of a horse. I looked in all directions to see who was making that sound.

'Subbu, it is emanating from the ocean and not from any one of us,' Swamiji told me.

Oddly enough, the whispering voices had completely vanished and now we could hear only the laughter.

'The decibels of this laughter will increase the more you think about it. Although it is going to be tough, try to concentrate only on the sounds of the collective chanting as that is the best way to dissuade that spirit from continuing with its irritating and scary laughter. This spirit is also trying to make you lose your focus on the beautiful vibrations emanating from the chanting. Let us not allow that to happen,' said Swamiji, who closed his eyes and re-entered into meditation.

# 37

# Swamiji's Arm Attacked

I saw Tantrayya carrying some dry wood and putting it into the fire. He made a few gestures with his hands, and suddenly, three flames rose to a height of twenty feet and then returned to the fire pit. Tantrayya ran towards me and told me to extend both my arms with the embossing on them facing the sky.

'The time has come for the transference to start!' he said, and turned towards Swamiji. 'Swamiji, we can start the process now. For this, all you will have to do is, just like Subbu, extend both your arms. The moment you do this, I have requested all the Aghori sadhus to start chanting the *Sushastra Parinamam* ancient texts. They not only know these but will recite them with powerful intonations and inflections. The recitation of these ancient texts especially by the Aghori sadhus will make the printed texts of the mantra on Subbu's forearms transfer on to both your forearms. This could take a few minutes, but will be quite painless for both of you.'

Swamiji gestured that he was okay with the plan of action. Tantrayya turned to the Aghori sadhus and told them to start reciting the Sushastra Parinamam texts.

Tantrayya had said that this process would be painless, but I could see that what was happening to Swamiji's forearms was extremely excruciating, to say the least. Although the view was not clear, I noticed a few large flies had suddenly perched on both of Swamiji's arms.

*Is this part of the process and if it is, where did they come from?* I asked myself.

Tantrayya was busy chanting along with his assistants and he seemed to be aware of this new development. To my horror, the skin from Swamiji's arms began to peel off but there was absolutely no reaction from him. It was as if those flies were trying to eat Swamiji's arms. I was not sure what to do. I could see the same syllables of the mantra form a print on Swamiji's forearms and at the same time, the carnivorous flies were gnawing at Swamiji's arms.

I called out to Tantrayya, but for some reason he was not able to hear me. Just when I was getting anxious about the whole thing, I felt a hand upon my back. I turned around and saw Sadashiv standing behind me. 'I was expecting this negative entity to try her antics here too but never imagined she would send flesh-eating vampire flies to hurt Shankara. She is doing this to stop the transference from happening,' said Sadashiv. He opened his woollen bag, pulled out his ivory conch and along with that, an enormous centipede. Seeing it brought back memories of my encounter with a similar looking centipede during my stay with the Aghoris in the North. Sadashiv told me not to fear the specimen and remain calm as the transference was still going on. He steadily moved towards Swamiji and in a flash, placed the centipede on Swamiji's right arm. The centipede quickly climbed towards the flies and started devouring them one after the other. Within a couple of minutes, all the flies had disappeared. Immediately, Sadashiv started blowing the conch and egged all the Aghori sadhus to continue the recitation and the chanting with higher intensity, and they did exactly that. Swamiji's arms were bleeding profusely but he seemed to be unaware of it all. Finally, the transference process concluded and Tantrayya indicated this.

'The process is finally over and it is truly glorious that it was completed successfully. All this was because of Swamiji's tenacity and calmness, especially going through the pain of having his arms being eaten by the flesh-eating flies. The entity who did this will face the consequences soon.'

'But what can we do to cure the wounds?' I asked. I was upset seeing the state of Swamiji's arms, and I wanted the healing to happen soon.

Sadashiv told me to step back and then, from his woollen bag, he pulled out two things that looked like small brinjals, albeit red in colour. He cut their tops off, and just as we squeeze a lemon, he did the same with the brinjals. After a few drops emerged from them and on to Swamiji's arms, he put them back into his bag. 'Shankara, by tomorrow morning, the wounds will heal completely. All you have to do is take me for a trek and then a swim tomorrow evening,' he said with a chuckle.

Swamiji was very calm, almost stoic. 'I will be all right by tomorrow; there is therefore absolutely nothing to worry about. I am most happy that the transference was completed successfully. I can see that Subbu's and my arms are looking exactly the same with identical embossing. I wish to sincerely thank Tantrayya, his assistants and the wonderful Aghoris who helped us with their awesome recitation. Sadashiv, if it wasn't for you and your help, this process would have remained incomplete. But more than ensuring its successful completion is the fact that you actually saved my life. The flies were hell-bent on eating me alive. I truly cannot thank you enough for all that you did to save me and the process. I am glad that you will be with us during the final extraction and transference process. Now, we need to get back to the temple because I wish to meditate on the new mantra before breakfast.'

'Swamiji, I also wanted to tell you that by tomorrow evening, the prints of the mantra that were formed upon your forearms through the transference process will begin to fade away and the same goes for Subbu. If permitted, I wish to meet you before the final extraction and transference to share this mantra to you,' Tantrayya said.

# 38

# Shree-Shakti Peeth

'Hey Tantrayya, when do you intend to initiate the final process and where is the location? Regarding our meeting, we can have that the day after tomorrow at 5 a.m. Will it be okay for Subbu and Sadashiv to join us?' asked Swamiji.

'Swamiji, there will be no problem if both of them join us. That's because I will be sharing the mantra privately with you, I mean the mantra will be shared in a volume and tone that only you will be able to hear. To answer your question regarding the location, date and timing, I will let you know during our meeting the day after tomorrow. I am still working on the planning of this extraction and that is because there is a possibility that, apart from Rishikesh, I may have to visit Kakudrayai forests in Sikkim to collect some wild flowers and herbs that I would require for the successful execution of the final extraction. But there is one thing that I need to tell you, Swamiji and Subbu. After the completion of the extraction and before the transference, the three of us—and hopefully with Shivaghori Sadashiv joining us—will need to travel to an Aghori cave at the base of one of the Himalayan mountain ranges. There is no official name to this mountain but we address it as the Shree-Shakti Parvat because the ancient Tibetan monks who were the early students of Lord Buddha had seen Shakti in a devi form on the mountain peak. Ever since then, this mountain has been addressed as the Shree-Shakti Peeth. It is at the base of this very mountain that an advanced sadhu known as Ashtaanga Sarvasiddhaya Mahaghori lives. A few even perceive him to be Lord Shiva, especially since he often is seen seated on the peak of Kailash completely naked in temperatures where one would need to wear at least three woollen sweaters.

'We will not just be seeking blessings but this entity, whom we also address as Harsiddhi, will share a few things with you, me and Subbu to enable the successful transference of the mantra. I hope you and Subbu are okay with this development,' he told Swamiji.

'As far as I am concerned, I will do anything and everything to ensure that all the three extractions and transferences happen effectively and successfully, and therefore Subbu and me will be joining you to meet this sage. I am also eager to meet him because it has been decades since I met and interacted with a great sage like him, and that too inside a Himalayan cave! Subbu, I am sure you will join me and I also hope my dear friend Sadashiv comes with us.'

'Shankara, you can surely count me in. I will be meeting the great Mahaghori after nearly a year. The last time we met was when some of us had climbed the peak of Mount Kailash in search of the elusive snow-serpent. One of the Mahaghori sadhus was captured by the serpent and I wish to know what happened to him.'

'So, it is done then. You are coming with us and my meeting with Tantrayya will happen the day after tomorrow. Also, Tantrayya will apprise us about the details regarding the second and final processes of extraction and transference. I need to say one more thing. Now that we are successfully through with the two processes, rest and lots of japa are needed for Subbu and myself and so, both of us—in fact, all of us—should spend more time in giving our mind and our body much required relaxation.'

Swamiji was right. I hadn't rested properly and was experiencing heavy-headedness and a bit of mental strain.

'Yes, Swamiji, I completely agree with you and I too will try to catch up on some rest and good sleep, and I will tell my assistants to do the same,' Tantrayya responded.

One of the Aghori sadhus stood up, bowed to all the people there and addressed Swamiji, 'Guruvarya, thank you for blessing us with such amazing opportunities to help you and Subbu make the two processes of extraction and transference successful. I promise you that we will also give some time to relax and calm our body and our mind. There is one technique I would like to show you some time and it is a technique we Aghoris practise to help us experience tremendous levels of not just rest but also inner peace. It is called *Vipriyashavasana* and for this, you need to hang your legs over a tree branch and then remain suspended for an hour. What is most important is that while in suspension one must practise initially *Bhastrikaya* pranayama immediately followed by *Sheetahalee* pranayama. You and Subbu can join us tomorrow.'

'What is your name?' Swamiji asked him.

'Srishti is what you can call me, Swamiji,' he answered.

'Srishti, I would love to experience this new and unique way of resting and generating inner peace; in fact, it could also lead to serene meditation. Having said that, we will surely join you but after the completion of the final process. I hope you don't mind,' Swamiji replied.

'Yes, sure, I will personally look forward to that after the process is completed,' he said and prostrated himself before Swamiji.

To personally witness such deep and selfless love for my guru from Srishti was truly soul-stirring. I was literally in tears and felt more reverence for Swamiji.

As everyone was leaving, I walked up to him. 'Swamiji, may I touch your divine feet?' I asked.

'Sure, Subbu,' he said and closed his eyes and allowed me to touch his feet. He then told me that he was very proud of me. He then stood up and we all left the place together.

## 39

# Bonding with Gomtee

I rested well and even tried doing the vipriyashavasana on one of the branches of the banyan tree. But it was of no consequence as, rather than getting inner peace and joy, I lost my balance and experienced pain. Fortunately, excluding a few bruises and a bruised ego, I was all right.

The next day, as I walked into the temple's cafeteria for evening tea, Ratnaiya ran up to me. 'Subbu, Swamiji has called you and it is urgent. I will ensure you are served your three cups of tea. Please reach the temple garden as soon as possible as they are waiting for you.' Even before I could ask what it was about, he ran towards the garden.

To be called by Swamiji was always the best thing to happen to me but the hurry with which Ratnaiya came and told me was a bit unusual. I immediately made my way to the garden and as I reached its entrance, I saw the enormous serpent coiled up and swaying its huge head from left to right. Then she suddenly turned around and looked directly into my eyes. Her human eyes and the eyelashes mesmerized me to the point that I began to get into a trance-like mental state. The next thing I knew I was seated beside Sadashiv and I saw Swamiji stroking the serpent's back.

'Is that Gomtee?' I asked. Of course she was Gomtee, but I was a bit hazy in my mind and it was probably Gomtee's hypnotic eyes that had caused me to feel disoriented.

Sadashiv said he had a solution to the issue. He told me to look at him and when I did that, he aggressively exhaled into my eyes. I quite spontaneously closed my eyes and when I opened them a few moments later, I felt absolutely no disorientation. I felt normal.

'Subbu, don't even ask what I did. Just look at them and the way both Gomtee and Swamiji are getting along!'

Sadashiv quickly joined them and a few moments later, Swamiji came up to me. He said that the bonding with Gomtee was very important especially for me as I was going to be envenomated by her during the extraction process. 'Gomtee insisted on this last night and was especially keen to have you bond with her. It seems like both of you have already bonded by the manner in which your eyes connected. Getting a bit disoriented is very natural as you have never seen a snake with beautiful eyes. I have already bonded with her and have felt her positive energy. Now it is your turn. I would like you to come with me. I will leave you with her and then I shall return to the temple as I have some meetings to attend.' Swamiji held my hand and invited me to join him.

I did as I was told and there was truly nothing for me to be scared of as I had seen Gomtee before at close range.

'Subbu, all she wants to do is bond with you and she will do that innocuously. Therefore, you don't have to worry about a thing,' Tantrayya said as I was getting closer to her. There she was with her gigantic girth and forty-five-foot length. She looked unreal but she was right there and very real. Her eyes were extremely calming and I spontaneously prostrated myself before her. She immediately raised herself and specifically her hood very high and this was a mark of her respect for me. That is what Sadashiv told me later. Gomtee then came closer to me and started coiling herself around me. I could feel the weight of her body on me but what was surprising was the fact that while she was wrapped around me, I did not feel an iota of fear. We were intertwined and we remained that way for almost three minutes.

After that, she unwrapped herself and slithered away to the temple lake.

'Subbu, the bonding process is complete. She seems happy to have bonded with you and is ready for the envenomation. I and my assistants have a meeting with Swamiji regarding the trip to the Himalayan cave we are planning. I believe it is time to leave and you could try to get some rest. But before that, remember that there are three cups of tea and some samosas waiting for you right here,' said Tantrayya.

He and his assistants left for the meeting with Swamiji and I went to my room carrying tea and tasty samosas. It took me an hour to finish the food and all three cups, and then I retired to bed for a much-needed nap.

# 40

# Beware Vampire Bats

The next day, as Swamiji had planned, we assembled at the temple. After offering our prostrations, we went to the terrace where Swamiji was already waiting for us. After chanting a Sanskrit prayer to Lord Shiva, Swamiji requested Tantrayya to elucidate the plan and strategy with regard to the extraction process. 'Sure, Swamiji, let me begin by stating the date for the commencement and completion of the extraction and then I shall share the same for the transference process. After deliberating with my assistants, we have decided to have the extraction on the sixth of next month which would mean exactly eleven days from today. Astrologically, it is the most auspicious day and I believe it is therefore the best day to perform the extraction. After checking, I have also come to know that the sixth of next month is a no-moon night or

*Amavasya* night, which also becomes very conducive for ensuring the success of the extraction. The duration of the entire process will be three hours. The process is quite long but we will have to endure it with all our mental strength and willpower. As regards the location, there has been a change. The location will be the Dhoomraketu temple deep inside the jungles of Bhatikala village. I have been told to conduct the transference in the same temple as it has the energy of Lord Hanuman, which means that for both the processes, Lord Hanuman will act as our protector as well as a keen observer. Apart from this, I wish to share one important aspect related to the extraction process. Swamiji and Subbu, please understand that there are quite a few negative forces and some of them are willing to go to the extent of killing you and even Swamiji just to ensure that the extraction process fails. These entities are not only doing this on their own accord but are going to be sent by one single person. She is a witch who is also very competent and she has some vicious anger regarding our dear Swamiji. She is trying her best to not let the three extractions and transferences happen successfully.

'I was truly not aware of this but was told about it by my seniors and this was confirmed by my brother, Tadamba. I have been, along with my assistants, chanting the *Guru-Raksha* beej mantra to create a protection for both of you, but just before this meeting, I got to know that this witch is planning to create extreme problems even before the extraction starts. She intends to hypnotize the vampire bats of the Yeliguri caves to come and bite you and Swamiji to death. Therefore, I earnestly request you and especially Subbu not to wander around, especially not into the forests that are on the outskirts of this particular village. I believe she has already done something to these bats so that they leave the Yeliguri forests and come here to cause all of us harm, but mainly to Subbu, so that we will be unable to either start or complete the extraction. Unfortunately, I and my assistants will be unable to do much to prevent these bats from biting us viciously and so I earnestly request you to endure the bites and the excruciating pain with all your mental strength. All that I can do is offer excellent treatment for the bites. Having said that, I have been led to believe that if there is one thing that can deter these vampire bats, it is an extremely high-pitched Sanskrit chanting and the vibrations that emanate from it. I am sure Swamiji knows this Sanskrit stotram but as regards Subbu, I would be very happy if he can learn it. I am saying this assuming he doesn't know it and I seek your forgiveness, Subbu, for assuming so.'

Swamiji said, 'Tantrayya, at the outset, let me clarify that I have not only heard about these vampire bats but also have been told about their semi-venomous fangs with which they not only bite their prey but suck their blood. But there is one more feature about these bats that only a few, especially those who have been bitten before, know about and I am one of them. Years ago, I had ventured to the Hridhay Nagin temple to initiate an extensive anushthana, not aware that there was a cave close to that temple deep inside the forests of Dadriyaal in the state of Himachal Pradesh. I was meditating when two of these bats entered the temple intending to feed on the temple's guard dog. The moment they saw me, one of them perched on my left shoulder and dug its fangs into me, as it wanted to feed on me. It was the quick-mindedness of my assistant that saved me from being infected deeply. He is now the chief priest of his village temple. His name is Shantana Bhat. He lit a fire as quickly as possible and shooed them away.

'The bite was deep and for a couple of days, I had to apply a paste that Shantana made using a few dead larvae of a special stick insect called *vish-taaniv*. This paste was applied every hour and to my surprise, within twenty-four hours, the venom had been sucked out and even the wounds caused by the bites had begun healing. It was now possible for me to continue my anushthana meditation with the same level of intensity. I can request Shantana to send me three bottles of this paste to help in the healing process in case we get bitten. Regarding preventing the bites, if there is one person who may know about that, it is my dear friend, Shivaghori Sadashiv,' said Swamiji, and he looked at Sadashiv.

# 41

# Sikunkaki Leeches and the Vampire Bats

Sadashiv prostrated himself before Swamiji, and after seeking his permission, he started with his response.

'Thank you Swamiji, for giving me the opportunity to share some of my insights regarding the vampire bats. Let me start by saying that there is a way by which we can prevent the vampire bats from even getting close and attacking us.'

'What is that?' I asked hastily.

'The vampire bats are extremely vicious and are also very fearless. The size of the human being doesn't deter the bats from biting them. I have seen a fairly large group of these bats attacking a large male elephant to the point that he died then and there from the attack. But if there is one thing that a vampire bat is scared of and will try and stay away from, it is the Sikunkaki leech and there is a special reason for it. This leech is the only creature on this planet that has a chemical in its abdomen which it can shoot three hundred and sixty degrees into the air. The mere contact of this powdery chemical substance makes these vampire bats fall dead to the ground within a couple of seconds.'

'What about the other animals and birds and what about human beings?' Swamiji interjected.

'Shankara, you will be happy to know that this deadly reaction happens only with bats, and that too only with vampire bats. With others, there is absolutely no chemical reaction at all. But we have to be careful as it is, after all, a blood-sucking leech,' he said and smiled at me and Tantrayya mischievously.

'Sada, how and from where can we procure these leeches and how many do we need?' Tantrayya asked with excitement. He was happy because he did not have to worry about Swamiji, me and him getting attacked and bitten by the blood-sucking bats.

Then Swamiji asked, 'Sadashiv, can we make some arrangements to get those leeches here and use them during the extraction? And can you tell us how exactly this would be executed?'

'That is not very difficult. I know a person who lives near the Aahoorayee rainforests not too far from this temple. That place is filled with these leeches and I will request him to get at least a hundred leeches to the location. I also wish to say to you and Tantrayya especially that the execution is extremely simple.

All that will be required is at least a dozen candles similar to the ones we use at home. These candles are available in any grocery shop. We just need to let loose the leeches on the ground and light all the candles in a large circular shape. The glow emanating from the light is very calming for these leeches and they will not be interested in climbing upon any of us. Also, the collective heat generated from all the burning candles will help prevent the vampires from getting close. Subbu, please remember you need to be extremely brave and prepared for any attack despite all the things that I have just shared. Your courage as well as composure during the extraction process will be key to it being successfully completed.'

'Yes Sada, you are right and to be honest, I have been through the first and the second process and at both times, Swamiji was personally present. This time too, he will be there and that is more than enough for me to maintain as well as enhance my composure and courage during the final extraction,' I said. I bowed deeply to Swamiji and continued, 'There is one more thing I wish to share with you. Just a few months ago, I not only lived but also travelled with the most ardent Shiva Bhaktas—the great Mahaghori and Aghori sadhus. The time I spent with each of them, especially from the time of the first mantra infusion, had ignited within me extremely high levels of fearlessness and the ability to handle myself in the toughest of situations. This time as well, I will have not only the five Aghori sadhus but at least in this life, I have a Shivaghori to reinforce this courage along with a sense of composure within me.' I offered deep prostrations to Sadashiv and the five Aghori sadhus.

Suddenly, Tantrayya stood up and walked towards me. He looked at me and told me that I was blessed by none other than Lord Mahadev and that I was the most appropriate person to have the mantras infused. He told me that Swamiji's decision to send me to the Aghori and Mahaghori sadhus at Kotisurya and then the Himalayas was something that Lord Mahadev himself inspired Swamiji to make, and that is how I had become such an integral part of all this. 'I am really happy today because, not only do I have two of the best assistants with me, but I have Swamiji, Sadashiv and the spiritual Aghori sadhus. In addition to all this, I have Subbu,' he said and hugged me. He had tears of love and affection.

Swamiji said, 'To all the people who have gathered here, I wish the very best for the successful completion of the final process of extraction and the transference. This process is going to start and could be the most dangerous for us as it is not just Subbu and myself who are participating in it. All of you need to enhance your spiritual and mental strength. Therefore, from today onwards, I urge each one of you to enhance and simultaneously intensify your meditation through whatever means possible. Subbu, I want you to enhance your japa and initiate the *Devi* stotram chanting every three hours every day till the beginning of the final extraction.'

'Yes Swamiji. I will start doing all of this from today itself,' I responded with a sense of grit.

## 42

# The Day of the Final Extraction

Just as we were about to retire to our rooms, Tantrayya requested us to sit. 'Our Gomtee has been waiting to see all of us and wants to hiss a hello!' Tantrayya began to whistle an extremely peculiar tune that resembled African tribal music. Out of nowhere, the large serpent slithered on to the terrace. She came directly in front of me and steadily raised her hood. She was so close that I could feel her tongue intermittently touch my face and especially my lips. Before I could even react, she hissed at me and then retracted and slithered to the place where the five Aghoris and Sadashiv were seated.

She was a couple of feet from them but was quite vigorously swaying her head from left to right. After a few seconds, she started raising her hood, just like she did when she was in front of me. But this time, she raised herself higher to a point where she was literally standing on the tip of her tail. I could not believe my eyes. At that very moment, Sadashiv stood right in front of her and immediately gestured to Swamiji to join him. The sight of Swamiji and Sadashiv standing with the serpent was surreal and spectacular at the same time. Albeit for a few moments, they kept staring at each other and I was sure they were saying something to one another. This went on for some time and then the serpent slithered away, leaving many of us wanting to see more of her. Tantrayya declared that she was happy to see us and that she would join us during the extraction.

In the time leading up to the day of the final extraction, Tantrayya went to his village and returned with certain ingredients for the process. I passionately practised the stotram recitation along with the pranayama breathing techniques. And finally, the day for the final extraction arrived.

I was excited and at the same time, a bit nervous. Yet, knowing that Swamiji and Sadashiv, the half alien Shivaghori, along with the five Aghori sadhus were going to be there to protect me through the entire extraction process was deeply calming.

Fortunately, the location for the extraction, the Dhoomraketu temple inside the Bhatikala forest, was not too far from our village. The arrangements were made for getting two sacks full of the leeches. At approximately 3 a.m., we left from the temple for the location. Tantrayya and his assistants were already there and were waiting for us. We reached the jungle and had to walk for about five minutes to reach the Dhoomraketu temple on foot. Tantrayya was waiting for us and the moment he saw us, he started exclaiming 'Har Har Mahadev' aloud.

It was half past three in the morning and Sanjayya came up, greeted us with prostrations and then offered us tea. A few sips and all my drowsiness vanished. Swamiji began to have an intense conversation with Kundali, the Aghori sadhvi. I stood in front of the temple and had a look at the place where I was supposed to be seated during the extraction process.

Tantrayya told me that he had let Gomtee loose in the forest so that she could roam about and simultaneously prepare for the task for which she had been brought here. He also told me not to think too much about her bite and the infusion of venom and that the queen caterpillar would do her bit to anaesthetize me.

'You will be absolutely safe through the entire process. The five Aghoris, my assistants and Sadashiv will be there to ensure that nothing will happen to you. Remember, more than all of us put together, it is the presence of Swamiji that will be the strongest protector. He is not only your guru, not only a realized soul but also one of the most advanced yogis living presently on this planet. The three powerful mantras he will have infused within him will then enable him to rise and become the most advanced and powerful sage among all the living beings here!'

I was not really scared of what I was going to experience but the reassuring words from Tantrayya truly heightened and further strengthened my confidence and conviction. I felt all the more blessed that I had the opportunity to do my guru's seva like this.

'Subbu, it is time to start the process and for this, I want you to have a cold-water bath and wear your angavastra. Will you be able to do this within the next fifteen minutes?'

'Yes Tantrayya, as requested by you, I have brought the vastra with me but where is the bathroom?' I asked.

Tantrayya smiled and replied, 'Subbu, you may have to take your bath under the waterfall behind the temple. The bathroom here has not been maintained properly and there are more insects there than fresh water. So, I feel it will be best to stand underneath the waterfall and have your bath. By the time you get ready and join me, we too will get everything ready for the beginning of the extraction.'

I immediately left and walked towards the waterfall. After my bath, I returned to the place where the process was to begin. I was greeted by Sadashiv, who said, 'Tantrayya and his assistants are almost ready. Tantrayya will personally come here and guide you to your seat. Subbu, whatever happens while the extraction is going on, please remember that we are there for you and will do anything and everything in our power to make sure the process goes off smoothly and you will be successful in completing it.'

As I was prostrating myself before Sadashiv to thank him for joining us and for his reassuring words, Tantrayya came along with one of his assistants. He took me to a certain spot and told me to lie on my back. He said that Gomtee would be here at any moment and I needed to start practising my deep breathing. 'Gomtee is extremely perceptive and therefore your calmness, which will happen through the deep breathing process, is crucial. It will also calm her down significantly. Please remember that even before her bite and the subsequent envenomation, I will be releasing the queen caterpillar for her to anaesthetize you. The queen will do it by leaving a gooey substance on your feet, arms and chest, and finally, she will do the same at the centre of your forehead.'

Just then Tantrayya's assistant Sanjayya started making some growling sounds and although I had laid down, I saw him slowing walking towards me, and along with him was Gomtee. For a moment I felt a bit nervous but the deep breathing technique that I was rhythmically doing was helping me remain calm and control my unwanted and nervous emotions.

# 43

# The Flames and the Serpent

Gomtee made herself a place to rest on just a few feet away from us and was quietly watching the final arrangements Tantrayya was making.

I saw a triangular-shaped *tika* (mark) on her broad hood. Someone had also applied kajal underneath her eyes, making them look prettier. Sanjayya then pulled out the box that had the caterpillars as well as another bag. He tapped the bag and within a few seconds, a pink cotton-candy type of thing came crawling out. Tantrayya told me that it was the caterpillar. He also requested me to stay still.

'Subbu, the extraction has been initiated and as a part of it, the first thing you have to do is remain still and try not to even twitch, as that will make the queen distracted and even disturbed, which may make her uneasy. She may even try to leave your body without releasing the gooey anaesthetic substance.'

'Tantrayya, I completely understand and I will do just what you told me.'

Tantrayya gave me a reassuring look and then quickly started making a paste of what looked like turmeric and rose petals. 'Subbu, this paste is being applied mainly to attract the queen towards the four points and, more importantly, to prod her to release the substance. I will also be adding some honey to the paste to create sweetness. I am going to apply the turmeric paste and also make you consume it to substantially improve your immunity to Gomtee's bite,' Tantrayya explained. He then applied approximately a spoonful of the paste at the four points where the queen caterpillar was going to release the gooey substance.

After doing that, he offered the honey-filled paste to me and I had a gulp of it knowing that consuming it would provide tremendous strength and a higher will to the muscles, nerves, blood vessels and, most importantly, to all my nerves to successfully fight the deadliest of infections that may be awakened. After swallowing the paste, except for feeling a tingling run through my entire body and especially through my spinal cord, I did not feel anything else explicitly within my body.

Sanjayya saw this happening and on Tantrayya's cue, he pulled the box close to him and placed it near my feet.

Tantrayya then opened it and I noticed a multitude of two-inch-long leeches wriggling out and settling themselves all around my body, with a few concentrating their positions extremely close to my head, next to my knees and some even venturing on top of my upper body. One of them tried to get close to the opening of my right ear only to be picked up and placed on my chest.

'Subbu, all of us are close to where you are, so you can rest assured of our efforts to protect you at all times.'

'What about Swamiji?' I asked as I was unable to see him.

'Swamiji is seated a few feet away from you. He is doing the *ati-shankya nusthana* or meditation for you and your well-being. And before you ask, Sadashiv is also here. He is seated on one of the branches of the peepal tree and will be there for some time practising *bhoot-bandha nishay* meditation. He will complete that and will be seated with the five Aghori sadhus who, as you can see, are seated diagonally opposite you and are doing the *akasha-drishti-havan* for your protection. The time has come for me to have the queen anaesthetize you at the designated points upon your body and after that, Gomtee will be infusing the venom into your body through her bite. Remember that while she is doing this, you may not feel any pain, which is a good thing. You truly don't have to worry about this at all as I have this under control. And hey, you may have your eyes open or even closed while all this is going on.' Saying this, he took a few steps back towards his assistants and whispered something to one of them.

Immediately, Sugandhim put large quantities of a fluorescent green powder on to both of Tantrayya's open palms. Tantrayya threw all of it into the air and began chanting a few verses of the *chandaal-nashtaha* stotram. As this started, he went close to the serpent and started stroking the back of her head. My eyes were open, thanks to my ultra-curious mind. Strangely, I was not scared at all, especially after the queen caterpillar had anaesthetized me the way that it was supposed to. I suddenly felt Gomtee actually slithering underneath my lower back and making a coil around my body. I kept my entire body completely still and my mind extremely calm so as to not distract the serpent. Gomtee's face was over mine. I was not sure what was going to be the next action, but within a few seconds, she moved away and towards one of the points that was marked with the yellow turmeric paste. She was staring at it for a few seconds and then, in a flash, she bit me at that very point.

By now the tips of her fangs were literally inside me and to my surprise, I wasn't feeling a thing. Gomtee did the same thing at the remaining three points and then slithered away into the forest. All this happened without any pain thanks to the powerful anaesthesia delivered by the queen caterpillar. I mentally thanked the serpent, the queen and also the leeches who had ensured my safety from the vicious vampire bats. But the extraction had only reached its mid-point!

## 44

# Speaking like a Serpent

'Subbu, the envenomation has successfully transpired and you will need to sit upright and stay there for some time. We have a few minutes for you to get ready to do this. Are you feeling the same as before the bite or different?' Tantrayya asked.

'I am feeling a bit dizzy but I think I will be okay once I sit up as you suggested,' I replied.

Tantrayya immediately offered me a brown leaf and told me to chew it for as long as possible. 'The dizziness means that the venom from Gomtee has begun to act upon you. I have given you the leaf as it will reduce the dizziness and at the same time, will speed up the effects of the venom.'

'Hey Subbu, I hope you are fine and aren't experiencing any discomfort or pain from Gomtee's bites,' said Swamiji. 'I have been deeply meditating for you to successfully go through the final extraction. I am also very relieved that, at least until now, the extraction did not face any obstacles and I do not foresee any until the end. Having said that, I am your guru and you are important to me. I, along with Sadashiv, will do everything possible to ensure the successful execution and completion of this process. Remember, more than even your guru, it is your Mantra Japa, deep breathing through pranayama and the mental chanting of the highly powerful Om beej akshara that will collectively strengthen you from inside.'

'Yes, Swamiji and, most importantly, it is my guru whose visions and memories of his love for me will truly ensure my safety mentally and physically.'

Swamiji gave me an affectionate smile and after wishing me well, he exclaimed, '*Jai Shankar*' aloud and returned to where he was seated. Just as this was happening, Kundali along with another Aghori sadhu came to me. 'Subbu, any moment from now, you will begin to hear certain sounds which you will have to tell both of us. Immediately upon hearing this, we will be writing it in our books,' she said. The other sadhu looked towards the dark sky and then they closed their eyes. Just at that moment, I heard a voice which was similar to that of the starfish, and all this was happening within my mind. Someone was saying something but saying it mentally. I was quite alert and listening attentively. Curiously, the voice was speaking in a language I didn't recognize.

Fortunately, all I had to do was repeat the words and I did just that.

'*Huyyeetee zauing zissmry mryutyamritam shadamass; raakhadree rakkth rahoo*,' I repeated quickly, accurately imitating the voice. This process went on for ten minutes. I did not have time to think much about what was saying all this. There weren't any visions or pictures of anything that was being formed. All that I was seeing were the memories of my trip to Mount Kailash and Lake Mansarovar and the circumnavigation of both along with Swamiji and a few others.

The voices faded away and as I was thinking that this was over, I suddenly started experiencing a lot of heat on my chest and forehead. Although the heat I was experiencing was not painful, it was quite unexpected and different. It was as though someone or something was sketching something on me and it was quite ticklish.

'Whatever happens, please don't move as that will disrupt this process. We need all these creations to be completed in one go without any sort of disruption or distraction.' It was Tantrayya and he spoke in a highly assertive manner.

I had never heard him speak in this tone, but then, he was very tense and I felt that there was a certain pressure he was experiencing to execute the extraction process successfully.

Kundali and her other Aghori colleague were busy viewing, analysing and then noting the same into their books. After that was done, they told me that the extraction was over and that each and every syllable of the mantra that was created through sound vibrations and also through body sketches had been noted.

'Are you saying that the extraction is over?' I reconfirmed this by asking Tantrayya who was standing next to me, getting the leeches as well as the caterpillar queen back into the box and the bag.

Sadashiv came up to me and told me that the process was still not over. 'Only after the collective chanting of the *Ghor-aghori* by the five Aghori sadhus as well as the mantra chanting by Tantrayya and his assistants, and finally the blessings by Swamiji can we safely announce the successful completion of this extraction.'

'Subbu, for all practical purposes, this process is complete and until we announce this formally, you may take a bath under the same waterfall and join me here. And one more thing, continue chanting your Mantra Japa just to deter anything or anyone from causing you any harm even though the process has been completed. These are words of caution and not of warning and so, do not get anxious or worried. We all will be awaiting your presence after your bath.' Hearing these reassuring words from Swamiji was deeply heartening and infused an extremely high degree of courage in me to face any or every obstacle.

As I stood beneath the waterfall, I could not believe that I had been through all this and especially significant was the envenomation part. It awakened a sense of positive anticipation within me for the final process of transference. As I walked back, I noticed that all leeches were gone and the Aghori sadhus with Sadashiv were waving their arms rhythmically and continuously exclaiming '*Har Har Mahadev*'.

Their voices were so loud that a few villagers came up to join them. These people were actually at the temple for the early morning prayers. Among them was a lovable old lady and she probably was the most animated in her love for Lord Shiva. She was dancing and encouraging others to join her. She happened to see me and quickly ran towards me. 'You are so blessed, my boy!' she said and offered me a white sweet. 'Here, please accept this prasad. I want you to have it now and in front of me, please. I have brought this for everyone but I would like you to have it first for all that you have accomplished here.'

I was feeling blissful with a sense of high accomplishment. I offered my gratitude to the lady and just as I was about to pop the sweet laddu into my mouth, I heard someone shout, 'No!'

The sound was so loud and stern that as an auto reflex, I froze. I realized it was none other than Swamiji who was galloping towards me.

He immediately pulled the sweet out of my right palm and after chanting something, he threw it away. Even before I could figure why he had done this, the 'sweet' that the old lady had offered me began disintegrating and I was shocked to see tiny maggots crawling out.

'Subbu, had you even put this into your mouth, you would have died within just a few seconds. I want you to go back to the waterfall and have another bath. This time, see that you apply extra soap to your hands and especially your fingers, and only after you wipe yourself properly, come and join us,' said Swamiji.

I looked around to search for the woman but she had vanished into thin air.

'Subbu, the apparently ardent devotee you saw was the wicked and highly dangerous witch, Soornayee, and she wanted you dead,' Swamiji said.

# 45

# Meeting an Extraordinary Sadhu

I was in a daze and rather than feeling wonderful about the successful completion, I was thinking more about the witch and how close I was to death. I had my second bath within a span of fifteen minutes and then quickly reached the place where Swamiji, Sadashiv and the others had gathered.

'Subbu, you have been instrumental in making this extraction successful and I also express my deepest gratitude to you for travelling to Kotisurya and going through the mantra infusion. Courageously and with your nishta towards your guru, you weathered each and every challenge, and I am very proud of you. Your work is almost done as the only thing remaining is the process of transference and a trip to the Himalayan cave to meet a very advanced Mahaghori. I am sure both these will be an enriching experience for you,' said Sadashiv. He pulled out a percussion instrument and started playing it in a way that made us dance.

Swamiji was standing near a tree close to the temple and had a smile on his face. The temple priest opened a box of sugar-coated cashew nuts and offered each of us a handful. After the spontaneous celebrations, Tantrayya requested his assistants to stack everything back into the bus, especially the bags of leeches and the queen caterpillar.

By the time we reached back, it was time for a few cups of tea. Swamiji went to his room and after a few minutes, I saw him entering the temple to conduct the morning puja.

That same night, Tantrayya, Sadashiv and I were called to Swamiji's room and it was decided that the four of us would travel to the Mahaghori sadhu's cave in the Himalayas two days later. Tantrayya also said that his assistants had already carried Gomtee and the queen caterpillar back. Sadashiv interjected saying that the leeches had also been taken to their respective jungles by his friends from the villages near those jungles. 'The reason I have suggested that we leave for the Himalayan cave a day later is to help us to properly execute the packing. We must understand that it is going to be the month of November and so, it will be very cold. What's more, we will be spending at least a couple of days inside the cave. We will need to get some warm clothes,' Swamiji explained and we agreed to his suggestion.

Endorsing what Swamiji had said and then re-asserting it, Tantrayya left Swamiji's room. Just as I was about to leave, Swamiji told me and Sadashiv to wait. 'Subbu, I understand that you are a bit confused and still stunned about what happened to you. Just remember that this witch is hell-bent on not letting the extraction and transference be completed successfully. When she failed to do this with the help of the vampire bats, she tried to do the worst, which was to end your life by tempting you with a poisoned sweet, and yet she failed. She has the powers and devious ones at that and will use them again either before or during the last and final transference process. The Mahaghori sadhu we will be meeting is going to bless us with a few things and I therefore want you and Sadashiv to be extremely attentive and alert to all that he says and does, which is related to the final process. If you feel like expressing a doubt or seeking clarity about something that he has said, do not hesitate to ask. This Mahaghori is no ordinary sadhu. He is one of the very few yetis who practises meditative hibernation beneath water bodies and inside caves. He has been doing this since the past twelve thousand years and most of it has been beneath Lake Mansarovar and on top of Mount Kailash. He is a highly realized soul and you will know that the moment you see his face and his extremely long arms.'

'Can you tell me more about him?' I asked and hearing this, Swamiji and Sadashiv noticeably looked at each other and shared a half smile.

'Subbu, we will share something with you about this great Aghori and a few other Himalayan sadhus, but now is not the time. We are very happy that the final extraction was completed with your amazing participation and now I want you to completely concentrate on helping in the transference of this mantra.' He then leaned forward and blessed me by stroking my back and the top of my head.

As planned, we organized everything for the trip with the main focus on getting some warm clothes. On the day of the departure, at around 5 a.m., Swamiji and I prayed to the temple deity and then left for the airport to head for Dehradun. Tantrayya and his assistants along with the five Aghori sadhus had stayed behind to sort out some more arrangements for the transference process and then joined us at the airport. After landing, we boarded a pre-booked vehicle and travelled to Rishikesh and from there we took another cab to a smaller town called Dhanglee. There was no motorable road from there to the cave so, after having some hot coffee with biscuits, we began to trek towards the Himalayan cave. Fortunately, we had hired some people to help carry our luggage, so we were able to trek comfortably. By evening, we reached the entrance of the cave and were greeted by a tall person who looked approximately thirty years old.

The moment Swamiji saw him, he ran and fell at his feet. 'Pranams to you, Swamiji! I am seeing you after close to four hundred years and you still look the same. Thank you for allowing us to visit you.'

'Shankara, it is only because of the blessings of Shiva that I am able to personally see and meet you in this life. I can see Tantrayya and my dear friend, Sadashiv, but who is the tall boy along with you?' he asked, with a lovely smile.

'Swamiji, he is my *shishya* (disciple) and his name is Subbu. I have brought him along as he is the person from whom all the three mantras were extracted. He will also be participating in the final transference,' Swamiji answered.

All of us were led into the cave and the man requested us to sit on the snow-covered floor.

I was a bit surprised to see a large chair there too.

'Shankara, you will sit here on this chair, and I will join Subbu, Tantrayya and my dear friend Sadashiv on the floor.'

As I sat down, I realized to my shock that not just the floor but the entire cave had become wonderfully warm.

'Are you all okay now?' the person asked, and Tantrayya, Sadashiv and I nodded a collective yes.

After we had settled down, the Mahaghori began addressing us.

'Shankara, I am aware of the extractions and the subsequent transferences of the mantras which your ardent disciple had brought embedded within his body a few months ago. You are at the cusp of the final process of the transference and this is where I want you to be aware of a few pertinent aspects that will help you be more aware and prepared. Subbu, you too are going to play an important role in the final part of this process although the extraction has already been done and your participation, especially your calm courage, is something I personally witnessed. We were all there, but not in the form you would describe as the body form. We were there in our astral energies and not in our physical forms. And by "we" I mean, along with me, there were also a few other Mahaghori sadhus during the final extraction.'

He then told all the others, including Swamiji, to gather around me. He signalled someone from outside the cave to come inside but I clearly remembered that there was not a single person outside. Then I started hearing a buzzing sound which kept getting louder with every moment.

Suddenly, a three-inch large wasp flew inside and perched itself on the Mahaghori sadhu's matted hair. We were unsure as to what was going on. I still thought there was someone whom he had asked to come inside.

'Shankara, meet the rarest of rare wasps. She will ensure no harm will come to you and Subbu during the transference process. Just so that you know, Tantrayya, his associates and, most importantly, your dearest friend, Shivaghori Sadashiv, have already met and interacted with this beautiful wasp. She has done this to each one of them and will do the same to Subbu and you.'

Swamiji closed his eyes. The sadhu then began making some clucking sounds and the large wasp with its dragonfly-like wings began flying to Swamiji and perched itself on top of his head. As it was seated on Swamiji's head, I could see it from an extremely close range and the sight was absolutely stunning. Although she did not possess human eyes like the serpent Gomtee, she was very different from the giant wasps I had seen in reality as well as in documentaries on television.

She was quite large in size but what was most stunning was her tail, which was more than half the size of her entire body. I also noticed that every second, a fluorescent coloured sting that may have been an inch in length kept jutting out from her body. Yet, she somehow had a very calm look, and I perceived her to be almost divine.

'Don't get fooled by her stunning and calming façade. She is a one-of-a-kind wasp who only lives here and inside the caves of the Himalayas. She may appear extremely calm but she is the most fierce creature I have ever seen. I have seen her biting and even driving a full-sized mountain lion to a painful death with just one sting. The venom she possesses is more lethal than that of the deadliest sea snake and at least fifty times more lethal than the black mamba. After Swamiji is stung, you will be next!' the Mahaghori sadhu said.

# 46

# Losing Consciousness

'I will be getting stung by a wasp that has been known to kill a mountain lion!' This thought gave me a painful sting. But I had no other option than to witness the goings-on.

Tantrayya and Sadashiv were seated alongside and comforted me saying that it was not as bad as I was assuming it to be and it was being done to ensure the successful completion of the final transference. I acknowledged their reassuring and deeply calming words and we turned our gaze towards the wasp.

The Mahaghori looked at the wasp and made some gestures in a kind of sign language that looked as if he was communicating with it. He then came and sat next to me. 'Just watch what happens now!' he said with a smile. In a flash, the wasp flew towards us.

The buzzing sound emanating from her wings was deafening. She perched again on the Mahaghori's head and after a few seconds, flew towards Swamiji. He was seated all along with his eyes closed and was in extremely deep meditation. The wasp landed on his right calf and started walking up towards his thigh. She reached there and immediately pierced her needle-like sting into his thigh. Swamiji twitched for a second and got back again into his deep meditative state. Within just a few seconds from receiving the wasp's deadly sting, Swamiji's entire body began changing colour to deep purple. To say that I was completely bewildered at the sight would be an understatement. It made me a bit anxious especially because his body was calm and Swamiji was not even inhaling and exhaling, at least that's what it looked like from where I was seated.

Fortunately, the colour began fading away and within a few minutes, Swamiji's body was back to its normal, resplendent skin colour.

'Shankara, it is time for you to lie down for a few moments and then, when you are fit enough to stand up, please sit next to Sadashiv.' Swamiji immediately stood up, walked to Sadashiv and sat next to him. The moment he sat down, the Mahaghori sadhu politely instructed me to stand up and come to him. 'Subbu, you too will have to undergo this and I am sure you will go through this just like your guru did a few moments ago,' he said and stroked the back of my head with a lot of affection. 'I want you to understand that what you are about to undergo is not only going to make you strong internally for the final process but will also help you enhance the intensity of the chanting of your Mantra Japa that your guru had initiated you into years ago!'

I nodded to express my acceptance and also to communicate that I was ready. 'Subbu, go and take your seat in the same place where Swamiji was sitting,' said the Mahaghori sadhu. I inhaled deeply, looked towards Swamiji who was seated with his eyes closed and after prostrating myself at his feet, I went and sat at the same place. Within a couple of minutes, I began hearing the large buzz of the wasp. I knew at that very moment she was not too far away. With my eyes closed, I continued my pranayama breathing process. I suddenly felt something on my head. 'Subbu, just continue to remain strong and silent. The wasp is seated upon your head. You just keep your mind steady by remembering your journey with me as we traversed Mount Kailash.' It was Swamiji speaking and he was trying to make me as calm and relaxed as possible. I felt the wasp slowly and steadily making her way towards the upper part of my back. Just as I was thinking about it, she stung me and I felt a shooting pain, and then I lost consciousness, at least that's what the Mahaghori sadhu told me later. I only recall waking up on a bed that had only silver feathers.

'Subbu, you have been here, inside this cave, for a few hours!' Sadashiv told me and added that

Tantrayya and Swamiji were near Lake Mansarovar searching for the *Oohureekayaa Spatheeka* within the lake and would be back before lunch. He also told me that the Mahaghori was very moved by the way I remained calm and composed despite being bitten by the Erongoad toad.

'What about that wasp? Wasn't I stung by her?' I nervously asked.

'Well, you were stung not by the wasp but by the Erongoad toad. It is a very powerful creature that does not belong to this planet. A species with a similar DNA lives on my planet but it is too docile and completely non-venomous. Having said that, the Erongoad toad is exactly the opposite and the gooey substance it carries upon its back is so potent that it can kill ten thousand people within just seven minutes. However, the same toad has certain substances in its front legs that, if applied to a human, can generate levels of immunity that are extreme and unimaginable to human beings. This toad did just that, which will make you absolutely immune to the worst kind of venom or other kinds of attack!'

What Sadashiv just shared with me was something I needed a few minutes to process.

Then, the Mahaghori and Sadashiv asked me to have dinner soon as we had a return flight to Mangalore the next morning.

'Subbu, the transference is going to be the final one and I am not sure if I will get to meet you again here, in

this cave. Therefore, I want to bless you from my heart.
Remember that I will be there whenever you need my
help. But never forget that you are truly blessed to have
Shankara whom you revere and adore as your guru. I
will visit both of you very soon at your village temple,'
the Mahaghori said. He dug his right hand into his
woollen bag and plucked out a red conch. 'Subbu, this
is a very unique conch, probably the only one that's
deep red in colour. I want you to blow it when you
reach the temple and believe me when I say it, I will
actually be able to hear it while I am either in my cave
or even from beneath the waters of Lake Mansarovar.
A few lifetimes ago, I had presented a similar one to
your beloved guru, Shankara. Just one last thing—
whenever you blow it, except for you, your Swamiji
and me, no one else will be able to hear it!'

I thanked him profusely and touched his feet, and
as I stood up with the red conch in my left hand, the
Mahaghori vanished.

'Subbu, you are a highly divine being and I
am honoured and blessed to have met you.' It was
Tantrayya and he was actually crying as he said this
to me.

## 47

# This Conch Has Life!

We were at Dehradun airport to take the flight home. During the security check, one of our bags was checked twice and then the head of security walked to us and asked if we were carrying an animal or a pet. Tantrayya stepped forward and assured him that there was absolutely nothing alive in the bag.

'Sir, there is a life force inside the bag and it was screened not once but twice. I will be screening it a third time now.'

'Sure, by all means. You may screen it even five times to check there is nothing alive inside that bag,' Tantrayya replied.

The head of airport security stood near the place where the screening of the bag was being done and the same thing happened. The screen again showed something alive inside.

'I will need to check this bag personally,' he said, pulling out the bag and unzipping it. With the help of his junior colleagues, he checked each and every part of the bag. They couldn't find anything alive. 'I am not sure what is happening. The scanner indicates something is alive inside, but we've checked every corner of this bag and there is truly nothing there.'

The head of security finally handed the bag to us and left with all his colleagues except one. He came up to Tantrayya and said, 'The red *shankaha* (conch) seems alive, but then this is just my hunch.' Then he left too.

Swamiji and Sadashiv smiled at each other and we eventually entered the aircraft. It was almost 11 p.m. by the time we returned to our temple. 'We have had a wonderful yet tiring journey back and so, I suggest that we get back to our rooms and meet tomorrow at 10 a.m. after breakfast. Sadashiv, if you are okay, I wish to have a few words with you after which you may retire,' Swamiji said.

I was very tired, so I had a quiet dinner in solitude and retired to my room. The next morning I was surprised to see Swamiji walking into the cafeteria to have breakfast. Tantrayya, his assistants, Sadashiv and I were seated together and having tea. 'Jai Shankar everyone! May I join you for a few cups of warm tea?' he asked. We prostrated ourselves at his feet and Tantrayya along with Sadashiv told him to join us so that we could discuss the date and location of the final

transference process. 'Oh, then we must also invite the
five Aghori sadhus to join us for the discussion. But,
for now, let us have tea and the crisp and tasty masala
dosa. Our temple cafeteria serves the tastiest ones, so
please enjoy it. Subbu, you must have had at least half
a dozen of them by now but you must have another six
along with me!' Tantrayya, Sadashiv and even some of
the temple priests seated at the dining table just beside
ours had a hearty laugh and continued to gobble up
the multitudes of masala dosas.

The breakfast was very tasty, especially the potato
masala that was being served with the dosa. I noticed
that even Sadashiv was having the masala dosas and
relishing every bite. I asked him about his carnivorous
diet and he told me that Swamiji had requested him to
forgo his forest-diet and develop a taste for the food
that the temple's cafeteria served while he was here
with us.

We completed our breakfast and by this time, the
five Aghori sadhus had joined us. Tantrayya suggested
that we should have the final transference process
on Monday as it was the day when Lord Shiva was
revered the most and we needed all His strength and
protection. Swamiji agreed and asked about the most
appropriate time for the process to begin.

'Swamiji, I wish to propose 10 a.m. as the time to
start this. The final process will be completed in an
hour and then my assistants and I will be performing
a very important fire-ceremony at the havan kund. For

this ritual, I have invited some of the advanced yogis and Aghori sadhus from the Himalayan region as well as a few who are going to come from as far away as Tibet. I believe most of them are already on their way and could reach as early as tomorrow morning.'

'Well, if that is the case, I will request them to attend the final transference. I shall also have arrangements made for their stay,' he said and looked towards Ratnaiya who gestured that the needful would be done.

'Tantrayya, there is one small request I would like to make. I understand that Gomtee is back at her nest. I am deeply of the belief that she should be present for at least the final fire ceremony and I say this because she played an extremely important role during the most critical process of extraction. Will it be possible to bring her here for it?' Swamiji asked.

'For sure, Swamiji. To be honest with you, I had already thought about this and sent my request to the senior Aghori sadhus there to help me in getting her here. The good news is she is on her way and will mostly join us the day after. Gomtee is coming here as she knows this place and just like a pigeon, she will navigate her way to this temple sooner rather than later. She will travel through rivers and mountains, therefore she will get here very fast,' Tantrayya replied with a big smile.

'This is great news to me and greater news for Sadashiv and Subbu as they are more enthusiastic about seeing and meeting Gomtee,' said Swamiji, looking towards us with a childlike smile. 'Now that the date and the time for the final transference process as well as the havan have been decided, I believe it is time to conclude this meeting,' Swamiji said and left to go to his room.

# 48

# Soornayee Is Here

It was Monday, the day of Lord Shiva. We assembled at the temple at 5 a.m. for the morning puja and Swamiji started chanting the *Daridra Dukh Dahana Shiva* stotram accompanied by all the priests of the temple. I contemplated joining them but was unsure about doing so. That's when Swamiji turned nearly 200 degrees, looked to where I was standing and then turned his gaze towards the idol of Shiva. I realized that he wanted me to start the chanting and not waste time on indecision. Taking a cue from Swamiji's silent stare, I immediately started chanting the various verses of this stotram. The entire temple was beautifully reverberating with the collective chants of the *Daridra Dukh Dahana Shiva* stotram.

After that was done, we also chanted the *Shiva-Manas Puja* stotram along with Swamiji and when that was completed, we went to the cafeteria for coffee. Swamiji and I were also served roasted cashews and walnuts. 'These nuts will provide us a lot of energy and strength—we both will need it if the situation gets stressful,' Swamiji said.

The final transference was going to happen inside the temple and near the same place where we had performed the early morning chants. Swamiji was the first to take a seat and then I was politely instructed to sit exactly in front of Swamiji. Sadashiv and the five Aghori sadhus sat in a semicircle around me while Swamiji was seated alone. He looked up and signalled Sadashiv to join him. Sadashiv stood up, quickly walked to Swamiji and sat beside him.

Seeking permission from Swamiji, Tantrayya and his assistants proclaimed that the final transference was going to begin with the five Aghori sadhus performing the *tukai-koochi*, a body movement done gracefully to ward off negative spirits and simultaneously invite positive energies to participate in the process. All the sadhus raised their right arm towards the sky and while doing this, they also lifted their left leg as high as their chest. They were also collectively making subtle, yet intense growling sounds. They repeated the movement more than a dozen times and then, after prostrating themselves before Swamiji, settled back to where they were seated. Now, it was Sadashiv's turn. Tantrayya made a subtle gesture to him and immediately Sadashiv stood up with his back erect. He started jumping six feet high in the air. He did this thrice and then started chanting something that sounded like '*Eekus kahouneeza shweap*'—it was a language unknown to me. I presumed it belonged to his planet.

He then prostrated himself before Swamiji and sat next to him.

'I will now initiate the process of the mantra transference,' he said and started pouring a yellow oily liquid on Swamiji's head. Then, he did the same thing to me. As that happened, a divine smelling fragrance engulfed the entire atmosphere. I closed my eyes and began inhaling it. All of a sudden, the fragrance that I was experiencing vanished and it was replaced with a strong stench of rotting flesh.

'Subbu! Don't open your eyes. Continue to breathe slowly and try not to get affected by this stench. This is proof of the fact that Soornayee the vicious witch is here but in a form that is unseen to the human eye. Stay as calm as you can. She is here to disrupt this process and she is quite capable of attacking any of us, but mainly you and me,' Swamiji said.

I tried to follow Swamiji's advice but the stench of rotting flesh was getting a bit too much for me to bear. I was beginning to feel suffocated. At that very moment, Sadashiv stood up, told Tantrayya to light a few incense sticks and give them to him. Sadashiv moved those sticks in an anti-clockwise direction and started uttering certain syllables, '*Yuong, rheenuong, sashaktaya nohamayaa*'. He kept saying this and within a few minutes, the stench faded away and the air was filled once again with the fragrance of the yellow oily liquid.

I thought Soornayee had left but then I noticed the assistant Sanjayya's body vibrating in an unusual manner. He began jumping up and down and then, to my utter shock he started pulling out the hair from his head in bunches and scratching himself vigorously. Soon, Sanjayya had no hair and he had started to bleed profusely from all over his body due to the incessant deep scratching.

'You cannot defeat me and I will not let you or this boy complete this process!' Even before Sadashiv or the Mahaghoris could react, Sanjayya or whatever had become of him ran towards a place where there was a fairly large-sized sickle. He quickly picked it up and came towards me. Just as he raised the sickle to cut my throat, the same wasp flew to his neck and stung him. Simultaneously, I noticed Gomtee raising her hood. She was exactly in front of him and in a flash, she struck his head. The moment this happened, Sanjayya collapsed to the ground and I actually saw a misty form leaving his body and zooming out of the temple.

'Tantrayya, we need to continue with the execution and the eventual completion of this process. So, I urge you to please compose yourself and continue. I assure you nothing will happen to Sanjayya. I will not let him and his valiant efforts die like this. For now though,

I would like this process to be completed. Sadashiv, I request you to ensure that the venom from the wasp and from Gomtee does not cause any damage and pain to Sanjayya. Please take him to a safe place and look after him. I know that nothing will happen to him. I will ensure that,' Swamiji said. He then looked at me and told me to remain calm.

Tantrayya took a few deep breaths and continued with the transference process.

# 49

# Agni Rises Again

The final process of transference had restarted with Tantrayya continuing his chanting and making hand gestures to the sky. I was seated in the same place, in front of Swamiji. My eyes were open and I saw that Tantrayya was unable to control his tears. Even as the tears rolled down, he passionately continued to chant and as he concluded, the mantra started transferring itself from my body and began moving towards Swamiji's body. Fairly large-sized flames in extreme white rose from certain points of my body and then each of them smoothly floated towards Swamiji.

The flames literally flickered all over him and then began entering his body through the midpoint of his forehead. Around seven separate fumes had emerged from my body and each of them was travelling towards Swamiji and entering his body. When it was time for the last fume to enter Swamiji, he suddenly opened his mouth, inviting the fume to enter his body through his mouth.

Once this process was completed, Tantrayya announced that the entire transference was finally complete. The five Aghori sadhus raised their arms towards the sky and began to chant 'Har Har Mahadev' a few times.

Swamiji slowly opened his eyes, extended his hands towards the sky and prostrated himself. Seeing this, I did the same and quite spontaneously started chanting the *Lingashtakam* stotram aloud. To my pleasant surprise, Swamiji also joined me and a few moments later, even Ratnaiya joined in. Although just Swamiji, Ratnaiya and I were chanting, it literally seemed as if a group of more than fifteen people were doing so. I felt so sure of this, I started looking around only to realize that except for the three of us, no one else was chanting.

Only later did Swamiji tell me that there were indeed more than the three of us but even though we could hear them, it was difficult to see them as they were in their energy form and a few were also present with us through the entire process in their astral forms.

The final process was now concluded and even though the Aghoris, Ratnaiya and a few priests were celebrating and rejoicing, Swamiji was trying to console Tantrayya. At that very moment, we heard the words 'Aulaakh Niranjan' being proclaimed at the highest decibel levels. We turned and saw Sadashiv and with him was the great Mahaghori sadhu who we had visited in the Himalayan cave. To our collective amazement, just behind them was the one yelling 'Aulaakh Niranjan' followed by 'Har Har Mahadev', and this person was none other than Tadamba. I could not believe my eyes. What stunned me more was that he was holding someone's hand and as they came closer, I saw that my dear friend Tadamba was guiding none other than Sanjayya towards the centre of the temple. Upon seeing his assistant, Tantrayya could not stop himself; he ran to Sanjayya and hugged him tightly.

He offered his gratitude to Tadamba. 'Don't thank me, it is Sadashiv and the Mahaghori sadhu from the Himalayan cave you must thank as they brought Sanjayya back to life. Had they not used the anti-venom, he would have passed away at the hospital. But Lord Shiva and the Goddess did not want that, which is why Sanjayya is alive. We brought him back because the doctors at the hospital told us that he has almost returned to normality. They are still in shock at the speed of his recovery and said that this was nothing less than a miracle.'

Swamiji immediately touched the Mahaghori's feet and profusely thanked his friend Sadashiv for being there for him through everything.

He said, 'Now that Sanjayya is here and so is Subbu's friend Tadamba, we must celebrate at the cafeteria with at least some tea, along with my favourite masala dosa and sambhar! But on a serious note, the formal completion of all the three extractions and transferences will only happen with the execution of the Agni Havan and this will be attended by a lot of people, including yogis and highly advanced spiritual entities. For this reason, I request all of you to be present for this event. With Tantrayya's permission, I would like to start the fire ceremony with my chanting of the powerful *Shankarashtakam* stotram and I wish that Sadashiv, the Mahaghoris as well as Tadamba and Subbu do so as well.'

'Sure, Swamiji. It will be a divine pleasure to have this chant uttered by you and the others,' Tantrayya replied.

He looked very happy especially because Sanjayya was back with him and looked as fit as he had been before being possessed by Soornayee.

Just as was planned, at night, we assembled at the place where the fire ceremony was about to begin. The fire pit was filled with well-oiled sandalwood and there were lots of petals of the kamalaswanki flowers. A multitude of incense sticks were also lit and they spread a refreshing and deeply divine fragrance. Just then Swamiji walked in and sat exactly in front of the fire pit. Tantrayya prostrated himself and then began adding the ghee. The moment he did this, the flames rose tremendously high, reaching heights of over 200 feet.

'Swamiji, you may begin the chanting and I will continue to offer the ghee and the other elements required for the success of this ceremony.'

Swamiji acknowledged this and after ensuring that all the people and yogis had assembled, started chanting the Shankarashtakam. Hearing him, I along with a few others also joined in. The entire place was reverberating with the vibrations emanating from the chanting and then I noticed a resplendent flame travelling towards me. In an instant, it touched me at the centre of my forehead, then it did the same to Swamiji and finally to Tantrayya.

The flame floated out of the temple leaving me in a daze. As Swamiji was chanting the stotram, another spectacular thing happened and I still wonder about it. Three flames from the fire pit rose extremely high and I think they rose even higher than 500 feet. But then, one of the flames did not return to the fire pit like the other two. It came speedily towards me, aggressively hit me on the top of my head and then immediately vanished. Even before I could understand what had happened, Swamiji looked at me and told me that Agni had blessed me through the flame and this was a very good omen for us.

The stotram ended at that moment and Swamiji requested Ratnaiya to give him the conch which he blew at an extremely high decibel.

'Swamiji, the sound of the conch itself will mark the end of not only this havan but also the conclusion of all the three extractions and transferences despite the challenges that Subbu and you have faced.' Tantrayya and his assistants, the five Aghori sadhus and Sadashiv walked to Swamiji and touched his feet, seeking his blessings and to my surprise, they did the same with me.

'To us, you are our true hero, a divine one at that. You not only brought back the three mantras but also participated in all the extractions and even the transferences with grit, absolute fearlessness and determination. It is for these reasons that you are and will always be our hero.' Sadashiv said all this and I could see his eyes welling up. What was amazing was that even Gomtee's eyes had welled up. I had never seen tears rolling from a serpent's eyes but I was not really surprised.

Tadamba, seated next to me, gave me a big smile. 'I will tell you more about Gomtee later,' he said, and just then we heard someone exclaiming '*Aulaakh Niranjan*'. Once again!

'He is finally here,' Swamiji said, closing his eyes and entering into deep meditation.

Scan QR code to access the
Penguin Random House India website